WILD WITCH

WILD WITCH
THE NOMAD WITCH™
BOOK SEVEN

TR CAMERON MARTHA CARR MICHAEL ANDERLE

DON'T MISS OUR NEW RELEASES

Join the LMBPN email list to be notified of new releases and special promotions (which happen often) by following this link:

http://lmbpn.com/email/

This book is a work of fiction. All of the characters, organizations, and events portrayed in this novel are either products of the author's imagination or are used fictitiously. Sometimes both.

Copyright © 2024 LMBPN Publishing
Cover by Fantasy Book Design
Cover copyright © LMBPN Publishing
A Michael Anderle Production

LMBPN Publishing supports the right to free expression and the value of copyright. The purpose of copyright is to encourage writers and artists to produce the creative works that enrich our culture.

The distribution of this book without permission is a theft of the author's intellectual property. If you would like permission to use material from the book (other than for review purposes), please contact support@lmbpn.com. Thank you for your support of the author's rights.

LMBPN Publishing
2375 E. Tropicana Avenue, Suite 8-305
Las Vegas, Nevada 89119 USA

Version 1.00, August 2024
ebook ISBN: 979-8-88878-689-5
Print ISBN: 979-8-88878-490-7

The Oriceran Universe (and what happens within / characters / situations / worlds) are Copyright (c) 2017-24 by Martha Carr and LMBPN Publishing.

THE WILD WITCH TEAM

Thanks to our JIT Readers:

Christopher Gilliard
Zacc Pelter
Dave Hicks
Diane L. Smith
Dorothy Lloyd
Jan Hunnicutt

Editor
SkyFyre Editing Team

DEDICATION

For those who seek wonder around every corner and in each turning page. Thank you choosing to share the adventure with me. And, as always, for Dylan and Laurel, my reasons for existing.

— *TR Cameron*

CHAPTER ONE

Scarlett Prynne woke at the insistence of the incessant beeping of her phone and sat bolt upright in bed. She had been in a deep sleep full of pleasant dreams of getting revenge on her brother for kicking her through the portal to Earth. Her sentient dagger Fang, which had been hanging on her bedpost, and her wand, which had been right beside it on the table, filled her hands. The dagger's concern flooded her mind, full of insistence that she explain the danger, but she ignored it as she blinked until her vision focused.

Runeclaw, her feline partner, had leapt up as well and looked no less alarmed than she felt. Scarlett dropped the wand, grabbed her phone, and growled, "This better be good."

Lin, the drow who was her best friend among the Witches on Wheels, replied with annoying wakefulness, "It is. Grab your essentials and get to the warehouse."

"What is—" The line had already dropped. Scarlett kicked her legs out from under the covers with a string of grumbled curses and jumped out of bed. After throwing on jeans and a T-shirt, she shoved her feet into her boots, strapped on Fang's sheath, and slipped the dagger against her ribs. She grabbed her leather jacket and revolver, then opened a portal to the Witches' warehouse.

As she marched through the opening, she slipped the revolver into the holster at the small of her back and forced her brain to settle down. The place was abuzz with activity, and most of the other Witches who were present looked as if they'd just been awakened as well. When she reached the office, Wren, the Witches' leader, and Amber, the Witches' infomancer, were staring at the computer screen. Scarlett asked, "What?"

Runeclaw jumped up next to Amber, and the infomancer absently patted him as she replied. "One of the college students taken by the Luminous Veil's lackeys has a medical problem that requires regular medication. They have an implanted tracker so their doctor can constantly monitor their vitals. The parent called the police to tell them about it, and I picked up the information from their system." The infomancer had a knack for finding data in all sorts of technically illegal ways.

Scarlett's excitement grew, manifesting as a butterfly flapping its wings in her stomach. "And?"

"And it's moved several times. Looks like they're portaling the woman and maybe the other captives from place to place. Probably standard procedure to throw off any pursuit."

"Where are they now?"

"Suburb of Boston."

Lin leaned through the door. "We've got a portal chain

ready. Grab some gear and let's go. Move your butt, Prynne."

Scarlett ran down to the arming area, ripped open her locker, and reviewed its contents. *First things first*. She didn't know how much time she had. She drew her revolver, flipped the cylinder out, and replaced the anti-magic rounds with one of each of the special ammunition types she had on hand. One anti-magic went back in, plus one shock, one explosive, one tranquilizer, and one incendiary. She rotated the chamber to align the anti-magic round with the barrel and shoved it in its holster.

Since Lin hadn't come to drag her away, she shrugged off her jacket, pulled on the harness that held her two long knives behind her shoulders, and donned the enchanted leather again. Her preparation time ended as Lin arrived with another Witch in tow. The second one opened a portal.

Through it, Scarlett saw another Witch and another portal. She and Runeclaw raced to keep up with Lin as she ran through both, plus a third. They wound up inside a tree line next to a three-lane road.

Lin pulled her forward as a car pulled up. "We're about five miles away."

They rode that distance and stepped out at the entrance to an interlocked series of streets with single-family houses on them. They paused only long enough to cast veils, then moved through the backyards with Amber guiding them through words in their earpieces and a map in their display glasses that showed sensor areas for motion detectors and cameras overlaid in yellow and red, respectively. It was simple to avoid detection with that assistance.

When they reached the backyard of the house next to their target, Lin opened a portal. Half a dozen Witches ran through, followed by a drone that swooped into the air.

Amber announced, "Stand by."

A small window opened in their display glasses to show the take from the drone's cameras. The neighborhood was quiet, which was to be expected at three in the morning, Scarlett supposed. One house had a small dot pulsing in it, the indicator for the medical tracker. She whispered, "How many do you think are in there?"

Lin replied, "Hopefully all, but maybe just her. It's worth it, either way."

"Can't argue with that."

Runeclaw had been mostly quiet during the preparation and travel phases of the operation. He offered, "I can check it out."

Scarlett replied, "We'll wait on Amber."

"Boring."

"You're boring."

He gazed at her with a sorrowful expression. "You shouldn't try to make jokes when you haven't had a good night's sleep. You're dumber than usual."

Lin laughed. "Cold."

Scarlett rolled her eyes. "See what I have to put up with? Everybody thinks it's nice having a cat for a partner. They don't know what a jerk he is."

Amber interrupted. "All right. I've got the house's alarm system identified and blocked. It might have a landline backup, but they'd have to turn the system back on to use it, so hopefully they won't notice. I don't see any other sensors emanating from that house, so you should be able to come in from the back without a problem. But there are a ton of low-level signals all over the place, neighborhood-wide, so it's possible I missed something."

Wren instructed, "Small team goes in first. Lin, Scarlett, Runeclaw. My team enters second. Teams Three and Four, you're here in case anyone inside tries to run."

Acknowledgments came over the comms. Scarlett murmured to Lin, "I can't see them running."

The drow replied, "Me neither. Portaling, maybe." She tapped her earpiece. "Based on the other moves, how long do we have before they portal again?"

Amber sounded uncertain. "Between ten minutes and an hour. But it's a shallow data set, so I can't predict with any real accuracy there."

"No time like the present."

Scarlett confirmed, "Just what I was thinking."

Wren ordered, "Go."

Scarlett had been holding her wand in her off hand since they left the car. She used it to solidify the force shields that covered her and Runeclaw and to ensure the veil that hid them from prying eyes and most sensors was up and ready. Then she let a small trickle of magic flow into her muscles to boost her strength and speed. When she was ready, she nodded at Lin.

The other woman nodded too and gestured for Scarlett to lead. The drow's magic didn't require any artifact to operate, so the bulk of her pistol filled her hand.

Scarlett reminded her, "Don't shoot the hostage."

Lin frowned. "But they said in that one movie that shooting the hostage was a good idea."

Scarlett shook her head. "I should've never let you talk

me into watching that movie. Although Keanu Reeves is cute, and I really liked Sandra Bullock's hair. Anyway, don't shoot the hostage."

"Fine. Be that way."

They advanced in a modest jog across the backyard to the rear door of the house. No alarms went off, and no lights came on.

Amber reported, "Still clear."

They crouched by the back door. Lin asked, "Quiet?"

Scarlett nodded. "Definitely."

Lin pulled out a set of lockpicks and used them to bypass the door's hardware. She twisted the knob, and the door swung open to reveal a darkened house inside. After they'd crept in and closed the door behind them, Scarlett whispered, "You take the upstairs, I'll take the downstairs."

The drow nodded.

Wren's voice came across the comm. "We're right behind you. We'll clear the main floor."

Scarlett nodded at the other woman. "Good luck."

"Be careful."

"You too."

Runeclaw yawned. "Boring. Let's go." He trotted off toward the stairs to the basement.

Scarlett suppressed her desire to yell at him and smack him unconscious and followed.

CHAPTER TWO

Scarlett had caught up with Runeclaw by the time they reached the door to the basement. The faint sounds of Wren and her team entering through the back propelled her forward.

Runeclaw darted past her and down the stairs when she opened the door, and she followed more cautiously. She didn't like him risking himself by taking the lead, but between the veil she maintained around him and his natural magical camouflage, he was unlikely to be seen.

Her steps were slow and quiet. Her greatest fear was someone triggering an alarm before they found the girl, and each passing second made that more likely. She wanted to run but fought the impulse and reached the bottom without incident. The staircase ended in a small room with a door to the side. She whispered, "Ready?"

Runeclaw replied, "Always." Scarlett threw the door open and surged through with her wand raised. The other shielded her eyes from the brilliant light in the next room.

Magic slammed into her shields, and she bolstered them as she took in the scene.

The furnished basement contained half a dozen people, three at the back of the room and the rest about ten feet away. The former consisted of one wizard and two people she recognized as captives from the most recent kidnapping. The latter, all men, had wands pointed at her.

A couch flew at her head from the side, and she sliced her wand through the air as she focused a thin line of force from the tip. It cut the couch into halves. Another quick force burst sent the pieces flying past her.

Runeclaw was already moving toward the back. He hugged the wall to her right, possibly unnoticed by whatever had spotted her through her veil.

She sent a blast of lighting from the tip of her wand, three prongs that reached out for each of the nearer enemies. The attack struck their shields and failed to penetrate as a portal opened behind them. She snarled a curse at the sight of it, then spat another as their magic negated the force wall she tried to cast to block access to it. A moment later, another wall popped up to keep her at a distance.

The momentary stalemate ended as Runeclaw attacked after getting behind their shields. He leapt onto the shoulder of the opponent farthest to her right and slashed his claws across the man's face. The man screeched, and the barrier faltered.

Scarlett ran through it and entered hand-to-hand range between the other two. She slammed a force-covered forearm at the one on the left. It met his magical protection, but the violence of the blow knocked him a step back, and he stumbled.

She slid her right hand into her jacket and came out with Fang. She dropped to one knee to avoid the blast of fire the wizard on her right sent at her and stabbed the dagger into her current opponent's calf. It penetrated his shields with no effort.

The man screamed, and a moment later fell like a puppet with broken strings as the tranquilizing poison in the sentient dagger's tip took effect. Scarlett felt Fang's pleasure and sensed more venom moving up from the reservoir into the tip.

The wizard on her right had darted away, out of range of a follow-up stab. She whipped her wand around and slammed a force burst into the wizard Runeclaw had slashed. A shout from one of the captives alerted her that they'd been pushed through the portal. She tried to snap a wall up in front of the other one, but it failed to materialize as the wizard herding the students blocked her efforts again.

A snapped, "Runeclaw, go," sent the cat dashing through the rift before it closed with the wizard and the captives on the other side.

Scarlett spun to the remaining man in the room, who gamely brought up his wand and blasted lightning at her. Her shields handled it with ease as she raced forward and stabbed him with the dagger. She was aiming for his arm but felt the dagger subtly twist as it went forward, as if she didn't have a good grip on it, and wound up stabbing him in the shoulder. She growled inwardly at the knowledge that the dagger had probably influenced her action again. That was a problem for another time.

She shoved Fang back into the loop that held it inside her jacket and forced her mind clear. She didn't know how long she'd have to make the connection and couldn't afford to wait. Scarlett sent her magic out, questing for the resonance of the pendant Runeclaw wore. She found it an unknown distance away, opened a portal to his location, jumped through, and held it as Lin rushed up behind her.

They entered a small concrete room with a garage door opening at the far end and rushed out into a long hallway.

Lin snapped, "Indoor storage facility."

Scarlett had seen the places but had never been in one. "Follow me." She felt Runeclaw not too far away and pelted down the hallway. She solidified her shields and strengthened them as she ran. When she burst around the corner and met a blast of magic from the wizard they pursued, it did nothing more than slow her progress.

Another wizard had joined him and was herding the students along the corridor. A portal appeared at the end.

Lin growled, "Oh, no, you don't."

Scarlett saw the force wall her partner summoned blocking off the portal and grumbled another curse at the fact that Lin could do what she'd failed to do.

The wizard in front of her seemed ready to fight, and after calculating the angles for a shot, she decided to oblige him. Her hand went back and drew her revolver. As she brought it forward and up, her eyes acquired the sight as it reached his leg. She pulled the trigger, and the anti-magic round passed unhindered through his protection and dug into the meaty part of his thigh. He grabbed the wound as he fell, and Scarlett blasted him with lightning as she ran past him toward the portal.

Unfortunately, her path took her into Lin's line of sight, and the enemy wizard chose that moment to cast a new portal. By the time they could react, he and his captives were through, and the portal was closing behind them.

Lin cursed, but Scarlett replied, "We're good. Runeclaw went with them." She cast a veil, opened a portal, and darted through with the drow a few steps behind. The room they entered felt like a trap, and she momentarily froze with alarm at the sight of eight people, plus the wizard they'd followed.

It took only a moment to realize six of the eight wore collars made of the magical metal, and the other two were the kidnappees. She snarled, "Captives," as she ran at the wizard. He sounded like he was done running as he shouted orders at the mind-controlled minions. They ran at her and Lin, and she shouted, "*Runeclaw.*"

The cat sent out a blast of lightning that encompassed all of them, but a shield shimmered around each. Scarlett still had her revolver in her hand. She flicked it to the explosive round and fired it at the magical, confident his shields would be up.

The round detonated when it struck his protective layer, and Scarlett used the moment to shove the pistol in its holster and draw Fang. When the smoke cleared, he threw a wave of fire magic at her. She blocked it with her shield and extended the cover to protect the eight captives as well.

She raced forward, accepting several force blasts on her shields as she closed the distance. The wizard realized his mistake when she was only a few steps away, and he grabbed one of the college students and threw her at Scarlett.

Scarlett had no option but to grab the girl and spin with her down to the floor, protecting the other woman with her body and magic as flames washed over them. The girl looked up with terrified eyes, and Scarlett flashed a grin. "Don't worry. We'll get you out of here."

The sound of Lin's gun firing repeatedly happened a moment before the barrage of fire lessened.

Scarlett looked up, saw where the man was, and grinned. In his effort to avoid the shots, he'd gotten too close to her. Using her enhanced strength and speed, she drew her legs up and threw herself forward in a lunge with Fang extended at full length. She only managed to scratch him, but with the dagger's venom, it was all that was required. He stumbled, tried and failed to cast a portal, then went down.

She turned to see that the other captives were all immobilized, either rendered unconscious by Runeclaw's lightning blasts or bound with force magic by Lin.

Another portal began to open on the far side of the room, and Lin snapped, "We need to get out of here."

Scarlett looked at the remaining captives, but there was no way to rescue them without another fight she doubted they could win. She created a portal, grabbed the two captives nearest her, and dove through, followed an instant later by Runeclaw, Lin, and a fireball that just missed her head.

CHAPTER THREE

After handing over the captives to the Witches, cleaning her gear at the warehouse, and showering back at the hotel, Scarlett portaled to Wheels. The others had said they'd meet her there. Lin, Wren, and Amber all sat at the bar. Scarlett took the empty seat in the middle of the group, and Runeclaw jumped onto the bar.

The Witch who was tending bar asked Scarlett, "Hard or soft?"

Lin replied for her. "Definitely hard."

The bartender popped the top on a bottle of beer and set it in front of Scarlett.

She took an appreciative drink, then blew out a long breath. "That could have gone better."

Wren replied, "The important thing is that you got the women out. They're at the hospital now. I just got a call from our medical folks who went with them, and they're fine aside from the stress and some bruises. One will be discharged in the morning. The other, the one with the existing condition, will be staying for observation."

"Do they have someone to keep an eye on them?"

Amber chuckled. "They have *everyone* to keep an eye on them. They'll be getting grilled by local police and the FBI for quite a while, I'm sure. Kidnappings bring down the full weight of the law."

Scarlett replied, "If only we could make it land on the right people."

Runeclaw interjected, "Maybe they'll mention us. We could become famous."

Scarlett shook her head at the cat, understanding the insult underneath his words. "Yes, and that would make life more difficult for us, which means I'd have screwed up again. I don't think they got a good look at me or Lin, and even if they did, I can't see them talking much about it. Also, shut up and let us enjoy the victory without your comments."

He laughed. "Touchy."

She raised a hand, palm out, and put it directly in front of his head so she could no longer see him. Turning to Wren, she asked in a forced, pleasant tone, "Did you find anything at the place?"

The leader of the Witches on Wheels shook her head. "Nothing interesting on the first floor. After you were gone, we took a quick look around but had to run for it before we could start a real search. They must have had eyes on the place because the police were on their way almost from the moment you went in."

Amber sounded angry, probably at herself, as she reported, "I didn't see anything or anyone." She took a drink of her beer, then added, "But we didn't have time for our usual planning. It's possible they had a drone or a veiled magical keeping watch on the place. Maybe even just a simple Wi-Fi I didn't pick up. In that signal clutter, it's certainly possible."

Scarlett reached over and patted the infomancer's shoulder. "It doesn't matter. That house was a waypoint, not a destination, and probably had nothing to offer. None of the bald baddies were present, just their minions. Guess they'll help with the capture on occasion but not with the mundane tasks afterward. Arrogant jerks. That's probably why they lost their hair."

Runeclaw asked, "So what's next?"

Wren replied, "We still need a lead, the one break that will split this whole thing open. It's out there. We just have to find it."

Scarlett thought about the blood on Runeclaw's pendant and what she'd learned from her sentient dagger Fang about using ritual magic to track it. The discussion had left her uncomfortable, and she'd been secretly hoping from the moment the girl's tracer had been discovered that it would make using the blood unnecessary.

Lin suggested, "We could surveil the house."

Amber drummed her fingers on the bar in annoyance. "Won't work. They won't be back. They'd only rented it for a few days. Everything was online, and they used anonymous accounts that are already dead. I checked it out right afterward."

Wren chuckled. "Hooray for short-term rental markets. Perfect for criminals."

Lin asked, "Any cameras nearby?"

Amber replied, "Some traffic cams, plus one on the store right at the edge of that little development. I checked all the feeds but found no sign of anyone entering or leaving the house. I didn't have a perfect view or anything and had to magnify and reprocess what I did have, but I still should've seen something if it was there to see. I'm guessing they went in under a veil the first time and portaled in after."

Scarlett growled, "Competent bastards."

"Seriously."

Wren's tone was thoughtful. "Think about this, though. We pushed them into acting more impulsively than they probably wanted to. It almost gave us something we could use. How can we do more of that?"

The question hung for a moment. Then Amber slapped the bar. Scarlett looked at her and discovered she was grinning. The infomancer answered, "Why, that's easy. Hand over what we know to the media."

Lin replied, "The police where the abductions happened will be furious. That could have some serious blowback."

Amber countered, "Correction. Give the media the information *anonymously*."

Everyone laughed, then Wren added, "I think it's a good play. Cover every possible thread back to us, though. No matter how tenuous."

Amber nodded. "I'll ask Glam to help."

"Good plan. Run your idea past Snow, too. He's an out-of-the-box thinker."

Runeclaw replied, "He doesn't even know where the box is." The unexpected comment made everyone laugh again, and the mood was lighter for a while. Wren and Amber departed, leaving Scarlett and Runeclaw with Lin. The cat curled up on the bar.

The drow observed, "I should probably figure out something to carry that I can use in the presence of others' magic. I need something like your darts."

Scarlett blinked. "Why?"

"I couldn't shoot the magicals for fear of hitting the hostages, and they had strong defenses against magic. Sure, I would've taken the shot anyway in an extreme emergency, aimed for their legs or whatever in case it went awry, but I need a better solution. Like your darts."

Scarlett replied, "We'll get you a bandolier and make some."

"I'm not great with thrown weapons. But maybe. It would be better than nothing, right? And I've seen you stab people with them now and again. I'm very good at stabbing."

Scarlett laughed. "Of that I have no doubt." She raised an eyebrow. "You could get Rath to teach you."

Lin raised both hands. "No way. That troll is way too intense for me."

Scarlett chuckled. "Why, because every other word is either 'must train' or 'chase me?'"

"Exactly. If you try to rest, you're doing something wrong in his eyes, I think."

"Well, we could all use a little more endurance."

Lin cut her off. "Okay. Shut up. Go away." She made shooing motions. "If you want to talk about work, go do it somewhere else."

Scarlett laughed as she rose and scooped up Runeclaw, who didn't react to being moved. "I need to get some sleep anyway. See you tomorrow." She opened a portal and stepped through to her hotel room, where she deposited

Runeclaw on a pillow and got ready for bed. Then she sat cross-legged on top of her covers and fell into a light meditation.

Runeclaw asked, "What are you doing?"

"Trying to see if I can connect to the blood through your pendant." She had placed a small protection spell on the item to keep the blood from being lost, with the thought that its placement on the pendant might prove useful. She sent her thoughts scouting out toward it and easily found the stone that allowed her to connect to Runeclaw.

Nothing happened when she tried to bridge from there into the blood and beyond. She tried it a different way, trying to bring sensations in through it, almost requesting rather than demanding information, but got no better result. After several minutes, she sighed, let the connection fall, and opened her eyes. "Nothing. Zilch. Zero. Nada."

"You're not good enough?"

Scarlett pinched the bridge of her nose. "Cruel but accurate, my friend. We'll need a ritual to do it, at least. Most likely, we'll need help."

He extended a paw and flexed it, his claws sliding out and back in. "Good that you're not too proud to realize it. Back to your village?"

Scarlett laid back and arranged herself to sleep. "No. I don't want to bring any heat down on them from the Luminous Veil, plus doing the ritual across planets is bound to be more difficult. If it's possible at all."

"Tinrorgan, then."

Scarlett closed her eyes and nestled her head into the pillow. "Yes. Tomorrow, we'll head to the kemana."

CHAPTER FOUR

Despite their many visits to the kemana under the city of Toronto, Ontario, Scarlett had not received permission to portal directly into Tinrorgan. She stepped through the rift from her hotel room to the security post outside the city with Runeclaw at her side. The giant Kilomea manning it looked her up and down, then nodded in recognition. "You are welcome. Behave."

She grinned. "When do I not?"

He gave her a look that said in no uncertain terms he suspected she was a troublemaker. As they walked past, Runeclaw loudly whispered, "He sees right through you."

Scarlett countered, "Shut it."

"Did you see the look on his face? He knows he'll have to clean up some disaster you cause."

"Stop."

"On the other hand, it probably alleviates the boredom."

She gave him a light kick with the side of her boot. "I swear, I'm going to portal you into the middle of a dog park and laugh my head off as you run for your life."

He sniffed. "Magical lightning works just fine on dogs."

Scarlett shook her head. "All right, quit being a jerk and focus."

They descended the staircase into the city proper and navigated the usual array of restaurants and shops. She found one she hadn't entered before and stepped inside on impulse.

A bell rang as the door opened, and an old man with copious gray hair on his head and chin smiled at her. "Welcome, my dear. I didn't think anything could be sweeter than my wares, but you have put the lie to that."

Scarlett laughed at the brazen flirting. "Oh, absolutely. I'm as sweet as they come."

Runeclaw jumped on the counter. "So sweet that milk curdles in her presence." The man laughed, and Runeclaw stared at him. "You can understand me?"

He nodded. "I have a cat of my own. Or, rather, he allows me to stay in my house, which he now rules."

Runeclaw settled back primly. "As it should be."

"Oh, of course. The natural order of things." He looked at Scarlett. "So, sweetie, what can I get for you?"

"One box each of the three things in the shop that you like best."

He clapped. "A woman of discriminating taste. Excellent." He went to several shelves and pulled things down, then set them out in front of her. "First, a box of the finest chocolates from Oriceran. They have fruit fillings with flavors not available here on Earth. A taste of home."

She grinned. "Perfect."

He set the next one down. "Nut bark, from here on

Earth, but with spiced chocolate. It's delicious, though a little fiery."

"Also perfect."

He displayed the third box. "But these are my absolute favorites. Hard candies, and each layer is a complementary fruit flavor. It's almost like eating a smoothie, one flavor at a time."

She shook her head, impressed. "I definitely came to the right place."

The man beamed. "So glad to hear it. Do you need them wrapped?"

Scarlett shook her head. "No, just as they are, thanks." She paid, promised to visit again whenever she came to Tinrorgan, and headed out.

Runeclaw asked, "Which one is for us?"

"None of them, unfortunately."

He gave a haughty sniff. "We should stop by Winter's Whispers."

Scarlett laughed. "No more catnip for you, not this trip. I don't need you tripping all over the place like last time." He grunted in annoyance and disagreement but didn't say anything more. They entered Ironwood, the shop owned by the dwarf, Jalor. She handed over the spicy chocolate.

He grinned. "What's this for?"

"A thank you. You've been really helpful."

He raised an eyebrow. "No strings?"

She nodded. "No strings. It's all yours. But I do have a friend who has a problem." She explained Lin's issue.

"Is she a witch?"

Scarlett shook her head. "A drow."

Jalor grinned. "Then I have the perfect thing. Wait

here." He bustled through a door into the back of the shop, then came out with a box about the size of a shoebox for boots.

He opened it and withdrew the item inside, a small crossbow, clearly made to be fired one-handed. "Pistol crossbow. Traditional weapon of the drow. This one was originally made by them, although I refurbished and improved it. It can now hold two oversized darts or quarrels in these stacked side-by-side chambers."

She examined it, pulled back the dual strings, and fired one. One was set above the other to allow them to be fired separately, or if one pulled both triggers at the same time, both would fire. "This is amazing."

"I agree. It came into my hands unexpectedly, and I'm happy to sell it to someone who can truly appreciate it."

Scarlett paid the price he named without any haggling and headed out.

Runeclaw asked, "Do you think she'll like it?"

Scarlett replied, "Maybe some. I think she much prefers guns. But she's right. Sometimes the old tricks are the best tricks, and it will fill the need for a nonlethal weapon. It's appropriate, anyway."

Her steps slowed as she neared where she'd met the witch she was looking for. The old woman had called her out on the street, mentioning she'd felt the power of her pendant. Her words had given Scarlett the clue she needed to start on the path toward unlocking the power her grandmother had left for her. She wasn't outside this time, so Scarlett knocked on her door and entered when told to.

The woman smiled but didn't rise from her rocking chair. She had thinning gray hair and a lined face, but most of the lines were from pleasure. The room was homey, like a house her grandmother had lived in for decades without changing the decorations. Scarlett offered her the boxes of candy, and the woman smacked her lips. "So kind."

"I have a lot to thank you for."

The old woman nodded with a knowing smile. "And?"

"I was hoping you might give me some information."

The woman leaned back, satisfied, and flicked her fingers at Scarlett. "Ask your questions, young one."

She managed to keep from frowning. "What do you know about using blood as a way to track someone?"

The other woman tilted her head and spent an uncomfortably long time staring at Scarlett from that position. Finally, she said, "I sense another presence among us."

"Runeclaw?"

The witch shook her head. "In addition to you, and I, and the guardian." Runeclaw straightened at being called by his title. Scarlett realized what the witch was talking about, reached under her jacket, and withdrew Fang. She set the dagger on the table between them. "This is Fang."

The woman extended a hand but paused. "May I touch it?" Scarlett nodded, and the witch rested three fingers on the dagger's grip. Her eyelids fluttered, and after a minute, she leaned back, opened her eyes, and rested her hand in her lap. She met Scarlett's eyes. "This one knows of blood magic."

Scarlett nodded, checked to be sure the woman was no longer touching the knife, then replied, "The dagger is powerful. I'd rather not become more indebted to it than I have to."

The woman raised an eyebrow with a look of extreme

seriousness. "I am also powerful." Then her lips spread into a broad grin as she laughed. "But my loyalty can be bought with sweets." Scarlett laughed, and the woman took a moment to unwrap one of the candies and pop it in her mouth. After savoring it, she asked, "Will the one you are seeking be watching for the attempt?"

Scarlett hadn't thought about that but couldn't see how it would be possible. "I don't believe so."

The other woman grunted and raised herself from the chair, her arms wobbling as she pushed herself up. "Very good. Then we will make this attempt. No time like the present since it's getting late."

Scarlett frowned. She'd entered the kemana in the early afternoon and had been there no more than an hour or two. "It's afternoon."

The other woman smiled. "Not where we're going."

CHAPTER FIVE

Scarlett expected the woman to gather materials, seek help, or almost anything other than what she did. Instead, she opened a portal and gestured at it. Scarlett stepped toward it, peered through to see a clearing in nighttime on the other side, and stepped across. Runeclaw followed and took up a position nearby, his nose twitching as he took in the scents. The woman closed the portal as she joined them, and with that light source gone, Scarlett's eyes adjusted.

The stars above and the moon slightly off-center overhead provided plenty of light to see by. Trees surrounded the clearing, which was an irregular circle of emptiness save for the one tree that occupied the center. That one was mammoth, clearly older than the ones surrounding it. Its gnarled trunk twisted and turned as it rose, and its bark looked almost like hardwood. The knots in it seemed as if they were faces and eyes watching them and judging their presence in the clearing. A sense of alarm accompanied the thought as she wondered what might happen if the tree found them lacking.

Scarlett drew her wand from her sleeve and cast the magic to enhance her senses. The surroundings came alive with tendrils of magic and a feeling of abundant, vibrant life. At the same time, it felt old, older than any place she'd ever been, and hit her awareness almost as if the clearing itself, or perhaps the tree, was sentient. Scarlett asked, "Where are we?"

The other woman smiled. "This is a place where the Good People gather."

"The Good People?"

"The fae. Fairies. Magical creatures that have always been part of this planet."

Scarlett nodded. "Ah." Then she asked again, "But where are we?"

The old woman laughed, seeming to take delight in confusing her. "Ireland."

"I have no idea where that is."

The woman's grin broadened, and she stepped forward to pat Scarlett on the shoulder. "Across an ocean from where we were."

Scarlett looked up. "Thus, the stars and the night."

"Exactly." The other woman took several steps away, then waved her wand and opened a portal. Instead of stepping through, she extended a hand across the threshold and came back with a jar that she set on the ground. She continued to pull items out of the air and set them down. Scarlett walked over and looked through to see shelves on the opposite side. "I've never seen a portal used like that before."

"Easier than carrying it all around with me. I'm not as young as I used to be, back when I was pretty like you, you know." She extracted one more item, then waved the portal closed. She handed Scarlett a cork-topped glass vial full of shimmering liquid. "Add a few drops of your blood to it, then put a dab on all the stones you can find."

The other woman knelt, took several jars, and headed for the tree in the center.

Runeclaw leapt to Scarlett's shoulder. "I can help with the blood."

Scarlett sighed at his eagerness. "Yes, fine." She held her hand up to him, and he scraped a claw along her palm. A few drops of blood welled up out of the thin cut, and she directed them into the vial, then put the cap back on and swished it around. The shimmering white became a shimmering pink.

She took it to the edge of the clearing, where she found what she'd expected to see, an irregular circle of stones that marked the outer boundary. She carefully walked around the perimeter, dipping her finger into the flask and putting a drop of the mixture on each stone.

By the time she finished, the witch had gotten all of her items to the tree in the center and was busily mixing things and applying them to the trunk. Scarlett spiraled in, looking for more rocks since the instructions had been "all" stones. She found about a dozen more in the middle ground, daubed them, and stopped when she reached the center. The witch paused what she was doing, touched her wand to her temple, and nodded. "Well done. Now, just wait."

Scarlett stood there, feeling impatient as the other

woman worked. She used the time to look up at the stars and search for constellations she recognized but saw none. She wasn't sure if it was because they weren't there or because she was too distracted and tense to notice them.

Finally, the woman instructed, "All right. Come here." Scarlett took a few steps dutifully toward her, and the woman tapped her shoulder. "Kitty."

Runeclaw jumped up to where she'd indicated. Scarlett would've thought that the impact would've toppled the slight woman, but she had a solidity that Scarlett hadn't noticed before. Or maybe she had it now but hadn't had it then.

The old woman held up her wand, then pressed the hand holding it against the tree to trap the wand against the bark. With her other hand, she touched the pendant around Runeclaw's chest. She said, "Now you." Scarlett set down the vial and copied the other woman. The old witch said, "The spell will take time to build and time to operate. Things might seem to move or expand around you, but have no worries. We are protected here. As long as we remain in contact with the tree, nothing can get to us, and nothing can hurt us. The Good People protect this place and those few they permit to use it."

Scarlett nodded. "I understand."

"Now close your eyes and focus on your connection to the pendant." When Scarlett reached for that magic this time, she found the witch waiting. Their magic merged, then pulsed out. It felt like it was expanding from the pendant but also as if it was flowing through her and her wand and into the tree. For a time unmeasured she stood there, all her attention focused on that throb of magic, the heartbeat of power, as it spread and spread.

Without a transition that she could notice, the heartbeat became a vibration. She sensed the solidity of the woman near her, the tree, and the earth below.

The old woman's voice echoed as she whispered, "All places are connected by the life that exists in the soil, the air, the water, and the people who overlap with all three. Through those elements and those people, we search for another trace of the blood that matches this one."

It might have been an explanation, or it might have been an invocation. It felt like both. Scarlett sensed lakes and rivers, then the enormity of an ocean. For a moment, she was lost in it, as if drowning, then she was moving without resistance, like she'd taken to the air.

A slight tug beckoned her on, and its strength grew as they moved toward it. Scarlett asked, "Is that the blood?"

The old witch replied, "At this distance, that's all it could be. If we were closer, the ritual might find blood connected to this blood, descendants, and elders. But it is too far for that." Again, time passed, an amount that Scarlett couldn't define. Then an image formed in her mind. It grew as if sketched by an artist's hand, first the barest outline lines in light pencil, then shading and thickening, then color.

The witch spoke in her mind. *Memorize it. Every detail.*

Finally, it resolved into a building. Scarlett sent, *I see it.*

Describe it.

Heavy stone blocks. Arches all over the place, both the windows and in the design. Looks like a ton of carving all over everything. I see flowers. Maybe faces. It's very clean, like it's well taken care of.

When Scarlett had finished, the witch replied, *I see the same. That makes this a true vision. This is where the blood that matches the swatch on the pendant is, or where it has been recently. Take a final look and engrave it in your memory.*

Scarlett complied, drawing upon every technique she'd ever learned to freeze the image in her mind like a photograph. It faded slowly at first, then like a bubble popping, it was gone. Her eyes opened in time to see the blood on the pendant crust over and fall away, leaving the gem clean. Catching her look, the witch explained, "We can only use it once because the magic consumes it."

Scarlett smiled. "May I hug you?"

The other woman laughed. "Of course."

Scarlett hugged her. "Thank you so much. I need to get moving to act on this. But I promise I'll visit the next time I'm in Tinrorgan. And I'll bring sweets."

The old woman laughed. "It will require regular deliveries to maintain my loyalty."

Scarlett laughed with her. "Consider it done." Then she opened a portal and stepped through to the parking lot of Wheels with Runeclaw traipsing happily before her.

CHAPTER SIX

Scarlett was surprised to discover Wheels operating at full capacity again, filled with locals and most of the Witches. She walked up to Lin, who was behind the bar, and gestured around. "What's up with all this?"

The drow put a root beer in front of Scarlett. "Well, it's two things. First, we don't figure we're likely to be attacked here again, at least not right away. And second, cash flow, you know? We need the local support to keep running, or we'll have to turn to thievery and outlaw-dom. Unless you've come into a sudden windfall and would like to donate it all to us?"

Scarlett laughed. "Hardly. I've almost blown through the savings I brought over from Oriceran."

Lin tossed a bar towel at her. "All right then, make yourself useful. Start cleaning up."

Runeclaw had been watching their interaction from the top of the bar. "I don't know that you want her handling fragile things. You might not have noticed, but she's kind of clumsy."

Lin asked, "Is that why you have dried blood on your palm?"

Scarlett held it up, examined the stain, and wiped it off on her jeans. "No, that's another story. I'll explain it in a minute. But first, I got this for you." She set the case containing the object Jalor had given her on the bar and swiveled it around so the hinges were on her side.

Lin wiped her hands on a nearby towel, then opened it. The drow's face brightened as she took the pistol crossbow out. She examined it from above, from the sides, and from below, then concluded, "Wicked."

Scarlett laughed. "You just called something made by the drow wicked? You don't get to say anything about me stereotyping ever again."

Lin had already drawn the strings back and pulled the trigger. A resounding *snap* followed. "Shush. Don't ruin the moment."

"It'll take the quarrels that are in the case. They're bigger than ordinary ones. Jalor said it should also fit the darts from my bandolier. Now you have the nonlethal weapon you wanted, assuming you don't shoot your target in the eye."

Lin took a minute to look it over again. "Big assumption, but I'm sure I'll be better with this than I am throwing the damn things." She put it back in the case with care and closed it gently. "Thank you."

Scarlett shrugged. "I owe you. Besides, anything that helps you helps me."

"Right on." The drow lifted her fist.

Scarlett bumped it. "Where's Amber?"

Lin made a vague gesture toward the back of the bar. "Her usual spot."

Scarlett wandered over and found the infomancer hard at work, as always. She sat in the booth on the opposite side. "Whatcha doing?"

Amber glanced down at her screen. "Searching every possible scrap of information we have on the Luminous Veil and getting exactly nowhere. How about you?"

"I might have a lead."

Amber met her eyes. "Really?"

"Really, really."

The other woman grinned. "Now we're talking. What you got?"

"A building. I can describe it for you."

"You consider that a lead?"

"I discovered it with ritual magic, tracing some blood from the last big fight that stuck to Runeclaw's pendant."

Amber's eyebrows rose. "Well, that's a different approach. All right. Describe it." Amber hit a few buttons and a flat plane appeared in midair, projected from her laptop.

Scarlett described the overall structure, and Amber drew it into existence with gestures. Scarlett suggested refinements as they went along, and Amber made the appropriate adjustments. After a short time, they had replicated the basic structure as she remembered it.

She added, "It had lots of thingies on it."

Amber laughed. "Thingies?" Different decorative elements appeared one after the other. "Like this? Or this? Or this?" It took about fifteen different styles before they found the one that looked right to Scarlett.

With that complete, they started working on color and other distinguishing characteristics. Amber's laptop chimed before they finished. A moment later, another image appeared in midair near theirs.

Scarlett pointed. "That is totally the place. You're amazing."

Amber grinned. "Driskill Hotel, Austin, Texas."

Scarlett looked at Runeclaw, who had been watching and occasionally batting at the hologram. "Looks like we're going to hit the road again, buddy."

He growled, "Promise me no stops at stupid places between here and the hotel."

Scarlett whined, "Aw, come on."

"Promise."

She stuck her tongue out at him. "Fine. I promise."

Amber said, "I've been thinking about some upgrades for Dusk Runner, and it probably makes sense to do them now if you're going to get on the road. Think Maddox will still be working?"

Scarlett shrugged. "Either working or cooking out behind the garage. I'm sure he'll be around and willing to help us."

They portaled to the warehouse to retrieve her motorcycle and walked it through another portal to the Spell Riders' garage.

Maddox was in his usual spot and tinkering with a motorcycle. He grinned as they approached. "Well, look what the cat dragged in. Hello, cat."

Runeclaw shook his head with a look of disdain in his eyes. "That never gets old. Ever."

Maddox laughed. "All right, grumpy. Let's head out back. I was about to break for some food, and you can join me."

Scarlett parked the bike, and they headed to the rear of the garage. Most of the Spell Riders were gathered around, cooking things on grills, drinking beer or soda, and generally relaxing. They joined in since Maddox didn't seem interested in doing anything other than eating at the moment and chatted amiably for a while.

Finally, he said, "All right. What did you come here for?"

Amber replied, "Upgrades."

Maddox slapped his hands together and stood. "Now you're talking. Let's get to it."

A handful of minutes later, Dusk Runner had replaced the motorcycle in Maddox's work area. He insisted on checking all the existing enchantments before talking about modifications. She and Amber did their best to be patient during the process. Finally, he asked, "What's your wish list?"

Amber replied, "One of the small drones I sent over a while back."

Maddox nodded. "Easy. We'll have to put a box somewhere on the bike to do it, though. Maybe on one of the saddlebags' frames. Is it okay if it's mounted vertically instead of horizontally?"

Amber shook her head. "No. It'll fall over before it gets airborne."

He waved. "All right. We'll figure it out. What else?"

"Enhanced remote piloting. Right now, I have the basics, but I want to be able to control what we add today.

I'd also like you to upgrade the servos to a more powerful version. Dusk Runner's a solid bike and the current ones are barely getting the job done."

He scratched his beard. "I was kind of afraid of that but had hoped the standard ones would work out. That's fine, but it'll take a while."

Scarlett replied, "Runeclaw and I have to get on the road tomorrow early."

"Won't be my first all-nighter." He grabbed some tools and started removing decorative pieces from the motorcycle. "Anything else?"

Amber replied, "It could use some weapons."

Scarlett looked at the infomancer. "Really? You'll have me driving a tank before you're done. Weight is an issue, as I think you mentioned just a little bit ago."

Amber countered, "So is survivability. If you're going to be off on your own, you need every advantage you can get. It's a worthwhile trade-off."

Maddox replied, "I can't argue with her. And I've got just the things."

He pulled out a sketchpad and quickly drew the bike on it as seen from the side, and another sketch of it viewed from the top. He circled the area between the handlebars above the headlight. "Double-barreled rocket launcher here. We'll disguise it as a design element. It'll have to be remounted each time, though."

Amber asked, "Fire and forget?"

Maddox shrugged. "Whatever you want to give me, we can load in there. I'll make sure it's fully interfaced with your remote-control module."

Amber replied, "Awesome." Scarlett grinned at the interplay between the two.

He drew boxes on the sides, right around where Scarlett's knees were when she was riding. She asked, "What are those?"

Maddox replied, "Needle launchers. You won't have any ability to aim to the sides, really, so we'll throw them in a cone and angle it downward. If someone's tire is nearby when you trigger it, it should be destroyed. If someone's riding a motorcycle next to you, well, that's not going to go well for them at all."

Amber chuckled. "Brilliantly lethal. I love it."

Scarlett shook her head. "Remind me never to let you two get together again."

They laughed, then Maddox drew a small rectangle at the back. Amber grinned. "Is that the Maddox special?"

He laughed. "You know it."

Runeclaw was sitting on the motorcycle's seat, making Maddox work around him. "And what is the Maddox special?"

He replied, "Caltrops. Little spiky triangle things that shoot out of the back."

Scarlett said, "That's seriously old-school."

Maddox nodded. "All the way back to the days of horse combat, yeah. At the latest. Some people say it was useful before that too, but I don't have any evidence that convinces me. Anyway, if someone's following you, this should mess them up good."

Scarlett quipped, "What, no rear-facing rocket launcher?"

He looked up from his drawing and asked seriously, "Do you want one?"

She raised her hands. "Nope. No. What you've done is good. All set."

He grinned. "I'll have it ready for you in the morning."

Scarlett looked at Runeclaw. "Guess that's our cue to get our stuff packed and ready to roll."

CHAPTER SEVEN

Shortly after sunrise the next morning, Scarlett and Runeclaw picked up the motorcycle from the Spell Riders and portaled back to New Mexico. From there, they hit the road to Austin. The day passed in a blur of enjoyable riding, stopping for meals and snacks, and looking at interesting things on the roadside. Scarlett might have exceeded the speed limit once or twice on the wide, open roads that connected the two locations from the sheer joy of being back on Dusk Runner, although whenever Runeclaw mentioned it, she denied it.

It was early evening by the time they arrived in Austin, Texas. The city was beautiful and seemed busy, with pedestrians everywhere as they pulled up outside the Driskill Hotel. The building was subtly different than the one she'd seen in her vision. From this angle, it appeared much more modern and in tune with the essence of the rest of the city.

Scarlett pulled her saddlebags from Dusk Runner, threw them over her shoulder, set the bike's enchantments, and wandered inside with Runeclaw. The lobby had a kind of Old World beauty, with dark paneling and brass lamps attached to the walls. A large square of ornate couches filled the middle of the space, with people seated on them talking animatedly about their day in Austin. They were loud enough for her to hear as she passed.

She smiled at the receptionist as she reached the desk and gave her name. As they did the usual dance that accompanied checking into a hotel, she slid a hand into her pocket, withdrew a small disc no bigger than a penny, and pressed it up under the edge of the reception desk.

The attendant handed over her room key, directed her to the elevators to get to her room on the second floor, and wished her a pleasant stay. As she walked away, Scarlett whispered, "It's placed."

Amber's voice came over the small earpiece nestled in her ear. "All right. I'll get started on breaking into the hotel's systems. I'll let you know if I find anything notable."

As she and Runeclaw waited for the elevator, they heard more talk from the group in the center. They seemed to be discussing ghosts, which caused Scarlett's mouth to quirk up in a half grin. She held back any further reaction.

Runeclaw waited until they reached the room, which was quite elegant in a way that matched the rest of the hotel's ambiance, then demanded, "You didn't."

Scarlett turned to him, her face the picture of innocence. "What?"

He narrowed his eyes. "You didn't book us into a haunted hotel."

She put a hand on her chest as her mouth made a perfect O of surprise. "This hotel is haunted? I didn't know that. What a weird and unexpected coincidence."

"You said you wouldn't."

"You said no tourist destinations between where we were and the hotel. I agreed to that. There were none."

He shook his head. "I hate you."

Scarlett laughed and fell backward onto the bed. "You love me." She bounced a couple more times on her back, then propelled herself up to her feet to unpack. "We should get a little shuteye or at least rest. Tonight, we'll prowl the halls and see what we can find out."

Runeclaw replied with suspicion in his tone, "About the man we're looking for."

Scarlett paused deliberately, then confirmed, "Oh. Yeah. Him too."

Runeclaw grumbled, turned in a circle on the mattress, then lay down. "If you cross over onto my side of the bed, I'm blasting you with lightning."

She laughed. "Probably fairer than I deserve."

Her alarm pulled her out of a deep sleep at three in the morning. A text message from several hours before reported that Amber hadn't found anything useful in the hotel's computer system. Scarlett rubbed sleep from her eyes and muttered, "Damn. I guess finding what we needed in the computers would've been too easy."

Runeclaw yawned. "Nothing's easy with you."

"Right back at you, kitty cat." She rose, debated changing into another pair of jeans and a different T-shirt, and rejected the idea. She slipped Fang's harness over her shoulders, slid her revolver into the holster at the small of her back, and put on her leather jacket and boots. She drew her wand from her sleeve and cast several spells before leaving the room.

As usual, she amplified her senses and gave a little boost to her muscles in case something weird happened. More importantly, she strengthened her connection to Runeclaw through the pendant. The blood was gone, but she hoped some minute trace of it might remain, and with their skills and senses working together, they might find the blood that had resonated with it during the ritual.

It was a long shot. They knew the man had been here, maybe even stayed here, but had no idea when. He might be here right now, or he might've left immediately after the witch had located him. She muttered, "Apparently I should've spent more time studying ritual magic."

Runeclaw replied, "And yet your fighting skills have gotten us through all sorts of challenges."

She looked down at him, surprised. "Did you just compliment me?"

"I was pointing out that some of your skills are less useless than the others. That's all."

Scarlett wiped imaginary sweat from her brow. "Thank goodness. I was scared for a minute there."

He gave her a condescending glare. "Shut up."

She laughed, cast a veil, and opened the door. "Let's go check the bar first. Maybe our friend stopped by for a drink."

They crossed the lobby carefully to avoid the staff handling cleaning duties and the one guest who seemed rather confused about how to find his room, walking around the lobby as if he couldn't find the elevator. She whispered, "He looks like he's had a fun night."

Runeclaw replied, "He looks like a chucklehead."

When they reached the bar's door, it was closed. She used her magic to manipulate the simple physical lock, and they slid inside. The room held a bunch of round tables that occupied most of the space, a few booths along the window, and a long bar that ran the length of the space. She said, "Be on the lookout for a cowboy."

Runeclaw jumped up on a table and stared at her. "I can't believe I'm asking this, but why should I be on the lookout for a cowboy, exactly?"

She answered with a wide grin. "Apparently the ghost of the owner, Jesse Driskill, still haunts this place. He lost ownership in a card game or something and is still upset about it."

"Do you really believe we're going to see ghosts?"

"I've seen a lot of things since coming to this planet that I wouldn't have expected. A talking cat, for instance." She poked him in the chest as she said it. "I wouldn't rule anything out." A thorough search of the room revealed nothing interesting, either natural or supernatural, and they headed back up to the second floor.

As they turned a corner onto the hallway across the building from theirs, they spotted a figure in a cowboy hat standing at the far end. A wreath of smoke undulated around him.

Runeclaw sneezed. "Cigar."

Scarlett advanced with slow steps along the corridor toward the smoky silhouette. "Doesn't feel like the guy we're looking for."

"No," her partner agreed. "Seems odd. Feels weird."

The figure turned his head toward them, smiled in a way that felt like an insult, and blew out smoke from his mouth and nostrils. It swirled out to obscure him, and as it vanished, so did he. Scarlett exchanged glances with Runeclaw. The cat asked, "Was that really a ghost?"

Scarlett shrugged. "I'm not sure, but we've been in the presence of the Good People. Why not a ghost?"

Runeclaw didn't answer, but Scarlett could tell he was thinking hard. They searched the third and fourth floors without seeing anything interesting. On the fifth floor, they discovered one of the doors cracked open. Scarlett muttered, "Okay, that's a little scary. This is supposedly one of the haunted rooms."

Runeclaw suggested, "We could just go back to bed, you know. We're guardians, not ghost hunters."

Scarlett ignored him as she pushed open the door to look inside. Shopping bags stood on the floor at the end of the bed, all slightly translucent like the cowboy had been. Neither of them entered the room.

Runeclaw asked, "What's the story here?"

"Two stories. The first says that a long, long time ago, a bride whose fiancé dumped her on the eve of her wedding killed herself in this room. Then, not quite so long ago, another woman whose relationship was ending ran up her lover's credit cards buying stuff, then also died in this room." A chill ran through her in a long shudder. "Good argument against relationships, if you ask me."

"Fortunately, no one will ever like you enough for something like that."

"Cold."

"I notice you don't say I'm wrong."

She stepped backward and pulled the door back to the mostly closed state they'd found it in. "Let's head upstairs." On the sixth floor, they spotted a woman in a Victorian bridal dress. Scarlett whispered, "She's probably one of the women from downstairs. What's she doing here?" She noticed this one seemed different than the others as they walked toward her together.

The bride vanished before they arrived, but Scarlett had seen a strange flicker from the corner of her eye. "Wait a minute." She created a few force steps and walked up them to the ceiling, where she pulled a small disc from its surface and examined it. "A projector. Not cool. They like being thought of as haunted. Let's go check the other places."

Runeclaw replied, "We're also not hotel inspectors," but followed her to the second floor, where they found neither a projector nor any sign of the cowboy. Inside the fifth-floor room, however, the bags were still present, and her quick search found no sign of a projector.

As she searched, motion in the corner of the room caught her eye. A woman who looked very similar to the one they'd seen upstairs, wearing the same wedding dress, stepped through the closed door into the bathroom. Scarlett ran over and opened it, but she was gone. She said, "So weird."

From his position in the hallway, just outside the threshold to the room, Runeclaw said, "So useless."

Scarlett blew out a breath through her nose. "Yeah, I guess so. But at least nothing attacked us, right?"

He replied, "The night is young."

As they headed back toward the staircase, they passed a painting she hadn't noticed before. She wouldn't have noticed it this time either except for the chill that crawled up her back as they walked by. She stopped and stared at it. It showed a little girl holding a bouquet in one hand and gripping a letter in the other. "That's just creepy."

"The feeling?"

"The feeling and the painting. Both."

Runeclaw replied, "Hmm." He seemed distracted, then a moment later, added, "He was here." He sniffed the air intently.

"What?"

"Our quarry stood here long enough that his scent is still barely noticeable. I guess he was impressed by the painting too."

The hope that had dwindled to an ember flared up inside Scarlett. "So we're on the right track." A yawn caught her by surprise. When she finished, she suggested, "Let's sleep. We'll pursue it tomorrow." As they walked toward their hotel room, she sent Amber a message to ensure she was watching the cameras. If he had been there recently enough that Runeclaw could smell him, maybe he was still in the hotel.

She looked back at the painting as they opened the door to the staircase and shivered. She'd seen strange things on Earth, but this place was stranger than most. If it provided a lead on her quarry, she would give it a five-star review.

CHAPTER EIGHT

The next morning, they had breakfast in the bar, which was also the building's restaurant, but saw no sight of their quarry or any additional paranormal guests. They checked out of the hotel and headed out onto the Austin streets with Runeclaw perched before her on Dusk Runner.

Scarlett had cast several spells before climbing onto the motorcycle, including a variant of what they'd done the night before. It wove the cat's and her senses together as tightly as she could and amplified them both.

Whether sight, smell, that vague inkling Runeclaw had of where magic wasn't working properly, or maybe some suggestions from the dearly departed who hadn't quite departed, she hoped their enhanced senses would be more receptive to them. It stung that she had no better plan than to drive the streets and wait for inspiration to strike, but sometimes life was like that, she supposed. Besides, it was a nice day and a new place, and exploring had always been something she loved.

They drove through city streets bounded by buildings tall and small and past impressive parks and a large university. Eventually they passed an imposing structure, and she commented, "State Capitol."

Runeclaw replied, "It's weird that it's not in the biggest city."

"Is it? I don't know how those things work here."

Runeclaw paused. "I guess I don't actually, either. But it *seems* weird, doesn't it?"

Scarlett laughed and patted him on the head. "It definitely does, my friend." They stopped at a small market and indulged in some ice cream, hers on a cone and his in a cup, then continued riding. When they encountered a beautiful building with a huge star on the front façade, Runeclaw remarked, "They like things big here, don't they."

"Oh, I think you could say that." It was another hour before she noticed a slight pull, a hint of desire to head west. Runeclaw mentioned it a moment after she detected it, and they turned in that direction to follow the feeling.

The sensation grew stronger as they wove through several turns, then stronger still as she pulled off the road into an industrial park. They drove past dozens of huge buildings, each with parking lots and assorted amenities, until instinct warned her it was time to proceed with more caution.

Scarlett pulled Dusk Runner into the shelter of the nearest building and activated its wards. She took off her jacket and added her knives and bandolier of darts to the other weapons she carried. None of them were visible with her jacket zipped up and her hair out of its ponytail. She cast a veil, and together she and Runeclaw moved across the neatly cut lawn in the open area between one building to the next.

She felt drawn to the second one they came to, and Runeclaw confirmed that he did too. The signage named a company she was unfamiliar with, and she took a picture of the logo and messaged it to Amber. Then she looked around for obvious cameras or sensors but found none. Runeclaw said, "Looks abandoned."

"It does. But is that because no one's here or because they want people to *think* there's no one here?" She jogged forward to an appropriate distance and patted her chest. "Time to fly."

He jumped up. She grabbed him tight and blasted force magic into the ground to send herself flying up to the roof of the building. She landed in a crouch and froze, sweeping her vision across the entire roof surface. Again, she spotted neither cameras nor sensors, and the signal detectors in her display glasses agreed with her assessment.

Amber spoke in her ear. "The company appears to be closed down. Bankrupt. I'm searching for additional information."

Scarlett replied, "Got it," and crept to one of the several skylights in the roof. It was convenient for sneaky people like her that so many businesses, or at least the architects who had designed the buildings, wanted natural light. She looked down through the window and immediately stiffened.

Runeclaw leapt to her shoulder. "Just like what we saw in the cavern."

"Yeah. There are the hoppers for the magical metal. They look at least partially filled. Maybe that's what drew us here." She couldn't sort out anything specific in the sensation, but it was as likely as anything else unless one of the hotel ghosts had led them here.

"There's stuff in the other ones, as well."

She looked and confirmed his observation. "If our guy was here, the question is, was it their last effort to make the collars and these are leftovers, or will they be back?"

"Hope for the best."

Scarlett toggled her comm. "Amber, we found another setup where they can make the collars."

Amber replied, "I found something interesting, too." A picture of a bald man appeared on Scarlett's display. "He's on the board of directors of the company that closed."

"Kind of a reach."

"What else do we have?"

Scarlett chuckled. "Fair."

Amber added, "I'll try to crack the company. You stay and watch until I can get some tech to you."

"Got it."

Amber tapped her comm to select a different channel. "Lin." The other woman responded immediately, and Amber instructed, "Pull a couple of surveillance packages and get them to Scarlett. She found an interesting place. I'll be running for the next little while. Have it ready for when I'm done."

Lin replied, "Within the hour?"

"That'll work."

"Consider it done."

Amber killed the comm and looked around the room to be sure she wasn't missing anything she needed. She was in the warehouse office with her recently rebuilt rig, sodas to hand, and snacks nearby. Since they'd moved into this location and her old gear had been blown up, she'd been improving her programs and hardware. She was ready to deal with whatever defenses a defunct medical supplies company might have. It was time to dance.

She cracked her knuckles and activated her arming room. The pure white chamber materialized around her avatar as her magic melded with the technology of her computer system. Everything looked the same outwardly, but nothing was. She had written new code, bought other fragments to repurpose, and generally increased the effectiveness of her virtual gear.

The suit, tie, and shoes were still black, and the shirt white. However, she had upgraded the fabrics' defensive abilities, and the shoes had knives she could extend at a thought.

She grabbed three pistols, one tiny, one regular-sized, and one larger than normal, and shoved them into her jacket. It still held far more than it should have been able to. She had redesigned each pistol against the possibility that a previous run against the Veil might have some connection to this one. It was always better not to reuse attacks enemy infomancers had already seen.

The canister of spiders went into its usual position, and she slipped several other objects into the jacket's inner pockets. The last thing to go in was the flashing device that could stun most opponents momentarily and sometimes erase their memories.

Before, her belt had been unadorned leather. Now it had loops about the size of shotgun shells all around. Amber extracted slender grenades from another pedestal and slid them into the loops. She chose multiples of lightning, shock, and explosive.

Finally, she lifted a cylindrical object that fit perfectly in her palm. A mental command activated it, and a sizzling blade of yellow energy extended from one end. Lightsabers had little to do with *Men in Black*, but why be consistent when the dark web was a bundle of anachronisms?

She grinned as she slid that into a loop next to the canister of spiders. Ready to roll, she donned the sunglasses and uttered the catchphrase, "I make this look good."

Her avatar instantly transitioned into the dark web, hurtling along a bright ribbon at high speed. It carried her to a destination where she could search dozens of restricted databases simultaneously, thanks to other hackers' efforts. She quickly found the company's network address and navigated to its location.

The company's access point appeared in front of her as a modern-day fortress, its entrance boarded up and protected by turrets, explosives, and guard dogs. A sign said the company had gone bankrupt, and its web assets were under the control of a government agency. It failed to specify which agency, which struck her as odd. Nonetheless, it meant she wouldn't get in through the front door.

Amber hurtled along a different route that sent her avatar weaving through other threads toward the larger buildings in the dark web's futuristic skyline. Her avatar landed with a small splash on wet asphalt in an alley between two tall buildings. She reached into her jacket, pulled out an orb slightly larger than a golf ball, and tossed it into the air. It hovered beside her head and cloaked her in a hologram that made her look like a character from a cyberpunk movie.

The illusion had purple hair sticking up in all directions on the half of her head that wasn't shaved. Her clothes were all leather and straps, her boots had studs up and down the outside, and she wore a pistol on her thigh in a holster identical to the one Han Solo had worn in *Star Wars*. Gaudy makeup that glowed strangely among the neon lights as she walked with a purpose down the street covered her face. Cyberpunk settings tended to be popular among infomancers, which was doubtless why this exchange had adopted one. She neither loved nor hated them.

Amber passed stalls full of people hawking information, code, or whatever else and ignored them all. She scanned the people around her in search of a certain person, someone she knew would be there, and finally found him sitting quietly at a cafe table, sipping coffee. She plopped into the seat across from him. "Look at you, all relaxed. I guess corporate work pays well."

He lifted a sculpted eyebrow in response. His face was Asian, but that was the only thing about him that fit into the cyberpunk theme. He wore a gray pinstripe suit, a bowtie, and a sardonic grin. "Selling corporate secrets pays well."

"That's good because I'm looking for one." She went on to explain what she wanted.

He nodded. "I have access to that information. It will require appropriate compensation, of course." He named a number and added, "Plus eight hours of work within a week."

Amber considered the cost. Part of his business was legitimate, and those promised hours might be spent on some aboveboard tasks. He might also use them for illegal tasks, and either one might strike her as amoral. She countered, "The money is fine. I need transparency on the job and the right to reject a task if I find it unsuitable."

Neither his expression nor tone changed. He'd doubtless expected a counter. "Acceptable. Make it ten hours, then."

She gave a sharp nod. "Done."

He held up a hand and flicked his fingers, which went from empty to holding a memory chip. She plucked it from his grip, and he pointed at a small booth nearby. "Slot it in there, and you'll be good to go."

"Thank you." As she rose and walked over, she restrained herself from pointing out that giving her a ride to the address was not the same as providing her the address. She had what she needed, so she wouldn't quibble about the details. Besides, she could always multitask on other projects while working for him as promised, which would be an appropriate taste of revenge. She climbed into the confining transparent cylinder, closed the door, put the chip in the slot, and dematerialized.

CHAPTER NINE

Amber's avatar rematerialized in a room that appeared to be a small lobby. A plasticky reception desk was on one side, a few cheap metal and plastic chairs were scattered around, and a large frosted double glass door stood along one wall. She released a line of code at the doors as she approached, and they slid obligingly apart. The room beyond was massive, easily the largest enclosed space she'd ever seen in the dark web. Some stadiums were bigger, but they were open-air.

The place was a blur of constant motion, reminding her of a video she'd seen of bees in a hive. Tall, narrow shelves full of products slid across the floor of their own volition while humanoid-shaped robots pushed large bins from place to place, occasionally snagging an item from one of the shelves as it flashed by. Other robots of different sizes and shapes whipped around at dangerously high speeds. She couldn't imagine the processing power that would've been required to make this place happen in the real world, given the speed of all the pieces.

The area was devoted to sorting data, but she couldn't assume it was innocuous or safe. Every computer system reacted to intruders differently, but in general they turned whatever was at hand to the defense of the simulation. That meant every robot, or none, might be an enemy, and she was sure other less obvious hazards would be sprinkled around the system since that's how she would have done it.

Amber stepped across the threshold into the room, ready to deal with whatever reaction it invoked, but nothing happened. A look up showed her that a similar amount of activity was happening at the top of the room, which had been blocked from her view. A grid of travel rails the robots ran along with their wares dangling behind them as they whipped around the warehouse constrained this part. She muttered, "Damn. This is insane."

A tap on her glasses activated a sensor pulse to investigate the room. It returned the shape of the space and a list of departments and their locations. All the usual ones one would expect in a modern company were present.

The one marked Research on the left-hand wall was tempting. Corporations always had such interesting and often illegal and dangerous things in the works. Since her goal was to figure out what was happening in the physical world warehouse and maybe get a line on the Luminous Veil, she'd have to set that destination aside.

The two departments that held the most promise were positioned right by each other. The first was Business and Finance, and the second was Logistics. Both would have records about the company's warehouses, and Business would probably have information on whatever transactions might have happened involving the warehouse after the company went bankrupt.

Amber summoned her disguise orb again to turn herself into a replica of the walking robots. An unused cart stood nearby, and after clumping to it, she pushed it in the direction she wanted to go. The departments were far across the vast warehouse, but distances were always strange within a simulation. It was equally likely to take her more or less time than in the real world, depending on how the system was designed.

As she walked, she slipped a hand into her jacket, which still felt like a jacket since the disguise was holographic. She pulled out her smallest pistol, which was tiny enough to be hidden in her robot hand. It was a newly developed device based on borrowed code and designed to disorient whatever it targeted. She'd coded it to pierce every defense she could think of and had confidence it would perform as well in actual use as it had in practice. Ideally, her disguise would get the job done, but it would be good to have the weapon in hand if that failed.

As usual, ideal and reality failed to line up. A robot moved toward her without a cart in front of it and without interacting with the stacks as they flew by. If it had a purpose other than her, she couldn't see what it might be.

When it was about fifteen feet away, she pointed the pistol at it and pulled the trigger at ten feet. A small disc shot out, flew across the intervening space, and stuck onto the robot. The mechanical man stiffened and wobbled as its steps stopped.

It stood motionless for long enough that Amber began to worry. It wasn't supposed to immobilize, and a trail of frozen robots would point out her presence to anyone watching. Then the robot turned and moved in a different direction, as if it had forgotten what it was doing. Amber allowed herself a small smile. *That* was how it was supposed to work.

As she continued across the room, she fired at every robot that approached her without a cart in its hands. She shot a few others at maximum distance to ensure anything processing the data from this portion of the simulation wouldn't notice a pattern of robots avoiding her. If they did see something strange, hopefully it would be attributed to a random element in the programming or an error.

Amber chuckled inwardly because whenever she thought of things like that, the notion of a ghost in the machine occurred to her, and she pictured one of the specters from the old Scooby-Doo cartoons she loved so much. If they unmasked the ghost in this one, it would be her in the costume.

She made it halfway across the floor before a different robot stepped out from behind a series of moving shelves. It took her only a moment to realize it had used them as cover to approach her. This one was half again as large as the rest, and its mirrored head showed the reflection of her avatar, which was deeply disconcerting.

A synthesized voice came from its helmeted skull and accused, "You do not belong."

She instructed her disguise device to constantly change the hologram around her in hopes of throwing off further pursuit and drew the middle-sized pistol from inside her jacket. It took only a moment to aim it at the robot's head and pull the trigger. A needle-thin beam lanced out of it and pierced the mirrored skull, shooting out the far side and into the air. The robot didn't seem to care, which made her growl, "Stupid." Of course it kept its brain somewhere better protected than its head.

Amber pressed the button on the side of the gun with her index finger. This pistol was her latest design and one she was particularly proud of. All the attacks that came out of it would be energy-based, but a randomizer inside would choose from a dozen variables to determine the nature of each shot. If an enemy created a custom defense against the shot she'd used, it hopefully wouldn't have one against whatever the gun emitted next.

She aimed at where its leg joined its torso and pulled the trigger. This time, a wide beam shot out of it to neatly slice through the metal. The robot tilted to the side, and she jumped onto it and used it as a launch point as it fell. She flew for only a moment, then grabbed one of the moving shelf units with her free hand and scrabbled with her feet until they found a hold on its shelves.

Amber aimed at the next security robot coming toward her and pulled the trigger. The same beam came out as a shield flickered into place to handle it.

She pressed the randomizer button and pulled the trigger again. This time, an orb of energy shot out of the barrel and flew toward the robot. The shield appeared. The orb angled upward to avoid it, then discharged energy down in a cone. The front-facing shield did nothing against this angle of attack. The robot sizzled as it went down.

A startled "Eep!" flew out of her mouth as she spotted

another shelf coming at her on an intersecting path. She dropped to the floor and dove out of the way.

Instinct took over from thought as more and more shelving units flew at her. She danced, dove, and in one case, ducked as two shelves collided and one went airborne. It was all happening too fast for her luck to last, and one struck her and sent her hurtling through the air.

Amber lost her weapon at the impact but landed in a stack of empty boxes near the packing area. The containers toppled down, and she tumbled with them. She landed on her back and noted her disguise orb was no longer with her, which meant she was back to her normal, noticeable look.

As she pushed boxes off and got to her feet, she noted four robots approaching. "Damn and double damn." She grabbed and primed two explosive grenades, then threw them underhand before bolting away in the opposite direction toward the departments she was still trying to get to.

They exploded behind her as she palmed two of the shock grenades and threw them back over her shoulders. Her feet pounded the concrete floor as she pelted toward the large garage door separating her from the Finance and Logistics section of the room. She didn't bother to check what was going on behind her. Her remaining smoke grenades flew back over her shoulders to add to the chaos.

Her glasses had analyzed the door ahead of her as she ran and determined there was no way she could hack into it since entrance required a physical component. She slid her hand into her jacket and came out with one of the extra objects she'd brought along, a flat disk like a Frisbee but smaller. She hurled it at the garage door beside the locking mechanism mounted on the wall. It struck the metal, then glowed red and burned through.

The door released and rolled up a couple of feet before something stopped it with a loud snap. She hit the floor and rolled through the opening just before the door crashed down.

CHAPTER TEN

The new area Amber saw as she rolled up into a crouch was entirely unlike the warehouse. The ceilings were far lower, and the corridor she'd wound up in was narrow, almost claustrophobic, with only two choices available. To her left was a door marked Finance. To her right, one marked Logistics.

Amber looked back and forth between them several times, then decided it was more likely that financials would be more heavily guarded. Even though the guards were programs, assumptions, biases, and instincts always worked their way into simulations. Logistics would probably be the less dangerous of the two.

She headed for the door and pushed through. Without visible transition, she was in a high-ceilinged space, although not nearly as large as the warehouse. The corridor she stood in stretched left and right, and another extended for a short distance in front of her. No markings or directions were visible.

Amber frowned at it, went to the left, and turned. More

choices awaited her, and she rolled her eyes. "A labyrinth. Exactly what I'd envision logistics to be." She let out a small chuckle and shook her head. "One point to you, designer."

She reached into her jacket and withdrew a small rectangle. She placed it on the wall she thought faced toward the center of the maze, then pressed its surface and stepped back. The brick unfolded, with pieces moving out in all directions before unfolding further. When the process was complete, the brick had resolved into a black rectangle the size of a standard door. Amber stepped back around the corner to protect herself from the detonation, then tapped her glasses to send a signal.

A loud crash signaled the explosives going off, and the entire space around her shook. The way the sound echoed gave her the impression that the room was annoyingly large. Still, if she could cut a hole through to the center, the size wouldn't be an insurmountable problem.

She stepped around the corner and stared in disbelief. The wall wasn't marred. Her door had done nothing. Amber frowned. "All right, another point for you."

She was a fairly direct person and had little interest in figuring out a way through the maze if her door wouldn't work. She'd take her chances with Finance instead. She returned the rectangle to her jacket, retraced her steps, and entered the door for Finance. She was thinking that the lack of security on the doors was odd when the door slammed behind her, and she took in her surroundings.

A loud groan escaped her. "Bank. Why did it have to be a bank? I've had enough bank experiences for one lifetime already."

The ceiling vaulted two stories above with a skylight set

in it. Tracks for large steel plates that would cover the skylight at night were visible on its edges. The place was abuzz with activity, with people dressed like figures from the nineteen twenties out for a day on the town. They moved from check-writing stations to teller windows or waited to be seen by one of the many workers arrayed in a grid of desks beyond a railing off to the left.

Again, this was all data or programs moving from place to place, interacting with other data and programs, doubtless doing the work of moving money around the corporation. This meant she was in the right place, even if she would have *really* preferred doing this in Logistics.

She reached back, dropped a couple of spiders from her canister, and sent them out to pick up whatever data they could. One never knew what worthwhile things might be lying around in the network. She had only taken a few steps toward the middle when an alarm went off. Steel barriers slid into place on the ceiling, gates came down over the teller windows, and the civilians ran through doorways in the walls. A few moments later, it was empty.

Amber reached into her jacket and pulled out the biggest pistol. A press of a button on the side caused it to grow and extend into a two-handed weapon with a grip on the front and another in the back. She sighted down the optics on the top and traversed the weapon slowly across the space in anticipation of the imminent response.

Two wall sections on the far side of the room slid out of the way to reveal gun barrels. She pressed the button to select rocket on her rifle and pulled the trigger to send a missile toward one of them.

She jumped and rolled to the side, using her shoulders

to control her motion as she hit the floor so she didn't lose the rifle. The turret she'd targeted exploded, and she popped up to shoot at the other one before taking evasive action again. The hasty attack missed and blew out part of the wall.

Amber snarled a curse, hit the button to reload, and released the weapon with her front hand. She reached into her jacket, grabbed a small tube, and lifted it at arm's length. A press of its button fired a grapnel attached to a cable into the air.

The magnetic disk on the end grabbed the metal shield over the skylights and the motor pulled her up out of the stream of bullets the turret sent her way. Her rifle beeped to indicate its reload cycle had finished, and she aimed it one-handed at the turret and pulled the trigger. The rocket shot out, and this time it hit the target, which exploded into shards that rained down onto the ceramic tile floor. Amber had only a moment to celebrate her success as more wall sections pulled away and a trio of heavily armored robots stepped into the room.

The robot nearest her raised an arm. She pressed the button to reverse the winch and descend, but it proved unnecessary as his first line of bullets passed through where she'd been and severed the cable.

Amber snapped, "Wing," and spread her arms as she fell, and her suit deployed cloth from ribs to wrists to help her control her descent. She landed hard but not as painfully as she would have without the suit's protection. She barked, "Cancel wing," as she dove to the floor and rolled behind one of the check stands.

Her inadequate cover exploded a moment later as a

rocket slammed into it. The impact threw her across the room and slammed her into a wall. If not for the protection she'd woven into the suit's fabric, a huge piece of the shattered furniture would have impaled her.

As it was, she felt the virtual equivalent of breaking ribs, not as painful as the real thing would've been, but still a distraction. In the physical world, it was a degradation of her connection to the system that would slow her reflexes and make everything she did from that point forward more difficult.

The rifle still held one rocket, so she pointed it at the nearest robot and pulled the trigger. The projectile flew across the room, giving her hope, only to hit an energy shield in front of the mechanical menaces and explode, dashing it. She snarled a curse, toggled the lever to switch the weapon's operation, and pulled the trigger again. Plasma bound into a cone shape by a magnetic beam lanced out and slammed into the robot. The shield that had been so effective against the rocket was useless against the beam, and her attack carved through the thing's chest as she moved the weapon in a spiral.

The beam fell off as its charge ran out. Amber threw the rifle away and dove for safety as two more rockets crisscrossed where she'd been. They slammed into the walls, which cracked and shattered at the impact. She swept a hand across her back to release the rest of her spiders as she got back to her feet and drew her flash device. She held it up and quipped, "Smile." When she pressed the activation button, bright light filled the entire space.

A wave of energy rippled out and slammed into the robots, which froze under the assault. Given that these were doubtless hardened models that had shielding over the components it normally might have burned out, she figured she'd only bought herself a few seconds. But that was all she needed.

Amber reached behind her back and drew the pommel from her belt as she ran. When she reached the first robot, she pressed the flat tip of the cylinder against its chest and activated it. A beam of energy shot out to create a sword. A diagonal slice took it down the thing's torso. Then she whipped it in a horizontal slash across the robot's legs to take it down.

Needing to act before the other one could adapt, Amber threw the energy blade across the room at it. It spun parallel to the floor and chopped through the robot's waist. It gave a sad electronic squeal as it collapsed in two pieces. She activated the weapon's return function and waved it in a flourish when it flew back to her hand. "A Jedi couldn't have done better."

A mocking voice accompanied the sudden sound of boots on tile. "I guess that makes me a Sith."

She turned toward the sound to see a man in a business suit, then reassessed. Man might've been putting it too simply. Circuitry created whorls and lines on his face, and his eyes glowed with an unnatural deep inner light. He raised a hand and beckoned her forward.

Amber snarled and charged, figuring it might surprise him. This was an enemy infomancer, and by his confidence and condescension, probably the one who had built the simulation. That meant he would be innately stronger within it than anyone coming in from the outside could hope to be and was probably wired directly into the server.

He became a blur of motion as she slashed and hacked at him, appearing to be in multiple places at once as he evaded the blade.

When her initial flurry ran out, he offered a sarcastic clap. "Wow. You're very good. If we'd met in your simulation, you might've even had a chance."

She politely replied, "Bite me," and drew a pistol with her free hand. She fired its electrical discharge and failed to hit him as he was suddenly on the other side of the room. She felt her spiders crawling around the system and figured she only needed a few more moments for them to get the basic information she needed. But he'd annoyed her, and she was determined to beat him.

Amber deactivated the sword and clipped the pommel back on her belt, put her pistol in her jacket, and pulled out a set of brass knuckles. She put one on each hand and beckoned him to come at her.

His laughter mocked her. If this had been her system to defend, in his place, she would've pulled a gun and shot the intruder. She'd read him properly. He was cocky and didn't only want to defeat her. He wanted to embarrass her. That, too, was a common trait of infomancers in their home servers.

He flowed forward at a speed her eyes could barely track and whipped an arm at her head that caught her a glancing blow as she stumbled backward. His kick connected with her chest and sent her flying to land hard on her back.

She somersaulted backward to her feet and charged him again, swinging a fist at his face. He danced to the side and gave her two punches in the back as she went by.

Amber groaned and went to one knee, stood, turned, and feigned a limp as she walked toward him. She managed to partially block his next blow but took another kick to the stomach and staggered back again.

Her opponent didn't know that with each impact of his fists or body on her suit, it injected code into his avatar. Each blow slipped in just a little, carefully portioned so it didn't activate any warnings.

The last blow had brought them to a critical mass. At her command, they combined into a virus that attacked his connection. His next punch was notably slower, and she blocked it with a smile. "Aw. Getting tired?"

The fist she planted in his face, augmented by the brass knuckles that cracked his cheekbone, intercepted his snarled response. Several more punches slowed him further, and she spun into a back kick. A mental command extended the knife in the heel of her shoe, and it sank into his neck as she came around. The blow took him down to the floor as blood gushed from the wound.

She pulled out her flash device and triggered it. Normally, his body would've begun to pixelate and vanish since she'd killed his avatar, but the device froze it before it could. She ran it over the avatar like a scanner, peered at it, and smiled. "Why, thank you. Getting the information from you was so much easier than having to search for it. Bye-bye."

Amber released him, and he vanished. She took one more look around, muttered, "I hate banks," and logged out of the system.

CHAPTER ELEVEN

Camus sat in his sitting room, ensconced in his favorite chair, and considered the long twisting path that had brought him to this moment. He'd fought hard to gain the status of leader and stepped in when the old one had died after making alliances and trading favors to put himself into position to do so.

From there, he steadily amassed his fortune and focused on establishing an iron grip on power within the Veil and on increasing the Veil's power in the larger world. Soon, that would all come together as the grandest plan any leader of the Veil had ever considered was finally realized.

He reached out, broke off a piece of the fruit and nut bars he treasured, and nibbled on it. The culling and capture were over, and they had enough subjects for his plans. He could've wished for more. He could *always* wish for more. Still, what he had would be adequate with a small margin of safety.

The truth was, losing even half of them wouldn't be

catastrophic. It would simply take longer to achieve success. His chin lifted, and his musings stopped as Ellis stepped into the room through the open archway.

His subordinate was dapper and well put together as always in his dark uniform. "Sir."

Camus waved. "Report."

"I brought another batch of collars for you to inspect."

"The ones I couldn't be present for?"

"Yes."

It had been a foolish question on Camus' part. Obviously, he didn't need to inspect the ones he had been present for since he'd been intimately involved in crafting those. If the other man had meant he only needed to add his spell on top of the others, he would've said so.

He saw the question in the other man's eyes but didn't intend to address it. It was not for anyone else to know, not even his most trusted subordinate, that he had begun to husband his strength like a miser with his coins. Crafting the collars was draining and also happened beyond the security of his home, his fortress. Neither of those things would serve him well now.

He had begun to think that since this was also the last opportunity he would have for a gathering, he might need to add a bit of magical persuasion to get people to take home collared servants, which would require his full strength. "Very good. They're in the basement?"

Ellis offered a short, sharp nod. "Yes."

"Perfect." Camus waited, but Ellis didn't speak. He just stood ramrod straight, looking uncomfortable. His employer pointed. "Sit. Have some coffee."

As Ellis moved to the chair opposite him, Camus

poured coffee into a mug and handed it over. The other man cradled it in his hands like it was a lifeline. Camus asked, "Any new information on the Boston debacle?"

Ellis coughed on the drink of coffee he'd been taking, collected himself, and set the cup down. "Only confirmation of our initial assessment. It was the witch and her friends, without a doubt."

"Vexing."

"Entirely. But the good news, if there is any, is we don't have a leak from within. The captive had a medical tracker that got a signal out despite the hardened walls. Very new technology."

Camus leaned back and sipped his coffee as he considered the new information. "How did we discover this?"

"Police records. First discovered by an infomancer, then verified with our contacts."

Camus lifted an eyebrow. "No doubts?"

Ellis shook his head. "None."

Camus spent a moment thinking, absently sipping coffee. "It seems wise for us to enhance our security, nonetheless. Add more guards to the collar forge prior to and during the final crafting session."

Ellis' expression was neutral. "Will you attend?"

Camus shook his head. "No, I leave it in your capable hands." Again, he noticed Ellis' expression, the unspoken question. If only they could have done the collars on the plateau, where he could've drawn upon the place's latent power to fuel his magic, he would have participated. In that place he probably could've done it himself. Building the apparatus there would have been too complicated since only the most trusted were permitted access.

After additional discussion of the gathering's details and the final forging session, Camus dismissed Ellis and headed to the basement. He found the box of collars exactly where Ellis had said it would be and noted with approval that one of the others had placed a magical lock on it to supplement the physical one. He cast the necessary magic to open the door to his private sanctuary and passed through, floating the box beside him.

He landed it beside his work area, changed into his robe, and sat cross-legged inside his ritual circle. After activating its protections, he went through his normal routine, clearing his mind, focusing his magic, and using this most familiar place as a touchstone to bring him back to his center. When that was complete and he was entirely present, he opened a tiny rift in the protection, reached through, and took a collar from the box he'd unlocked before activating the wards.

He held the thin metal circle in his hands and began to examine it. First, he ran his fingers along the collar, his magically enhanced senses searching for any impurity or flaw. Any flaw in the collar's physical form was unacceptable since it would be a vulnerable spot where the magic inside would eat away at the collar's structural integrity. After one such damaged collar had exploded during the research process, he'd refined their process from top to bottom to ensure strict tolerances.

Having verified its physical perfection, Camus took a deep breath and sent his magic spiraling into the collar. The initial interior examination was a mirror of the previous one. His enhanced magical senses moved slowly around the collar in search of any imperfections in its physical form. It was tempting to get lost in the fascinating way the metals twined and separated through the collar. Even though they had all come together, they had not merged into a unified substance. Instead, magic had held them separate and wound them into precise shapes and arrangements. It was a thing of beauty in form and function.

When he completed his circuit, he was confident the physical form was as it should be. Next, he tuned his magic to resonate with the base spells that held the physical form together. He perceived them as channels inside the collar's physical form. He zoomed the image in to allow him to examine it in fine detail.

The spells that kept the two key metals from touching were where they should be, as were the ones that kept the other metals in balance with the magical ones. He grunted in satisfaction. The collar was physically perfect. He'd expected nothing less.

He focused next on the magic trapped within the collar. The first spell was the one that acted upon the will of the wearer to destroy their resistance and make them susceptible to magical suggestion. That spell was as it should be. The next layer of spells were the ones that influenced the wearer after the first had broken down their defenses. He checked it carefully, component by component, and discovered something that wasn't quite right.

Camus frowned. The sensation was like a taste at the edge of his senses, something slightly rotten, slightly off. He investigated it more closely and discovered that one of the others had threaded a small instruction that would cause the wearer to listen to that person's suggestions more than others.

He scowled at the discovery. Even though he'd anticipated this, it was still frustrating to see it happen. It meant disloyalty. It also meant his plan to eliminate the others immediately after the gathering was a good one.

Banishing the emotion and finding his center again, Camus went to work on the spell and carefully untangled the threads that made it work. When he was done, the spell still appeared to be in place and unchanged but had been dramatically weakened. No one would detect the changes he'd made until it was far too late to do anything about it, but it would ensure the other's commands would not override his.

Finally, he moved on to the most important part of the night's work. He summoned his magic and wove it into the tiniest of openings in the collar, slipping it into places so small they were virtually undetectable. He chanted as he worked and drew sigils in the air with his wand.

Glowing lines appeared in the air, only to be sucked into the collar as he altered its magic. When he finished some unknown amount of time later, the collar had been primed to accept only his commands and to radiate them inward and outward at his discretion. That spell was his alone, and while he knew the others resented him adding magic he didn't share with them, it was of no concern. He was the leader. He didn't explain.

As he pulled his mind from the collar, his work complete, he took a deep breath and released it slowly. The fools thought they could get away with something while he wasn't there to watch over them. Well, that was easily handled. He couldn't detect who had done it, but he would warn Ellis to watch carefully during the next crafting session. Perhaps the culprit would give themselves away during the construction.

Turning his attention back to the collars, he opened the gap in the defenses, exchanged the finished collar for the next one he needed to inspect, and brought it inside. It would be a long night, but his path to power would be that much more secure when he finished.

CHAPTER TWELVE

Scarlett walked into Wheels and smiled at the ordinariness of it. The local clientele had returned in full, and everyone seemed relaxed and happy. A closer look allowed her to note the Witches positioned strategically throughout the place, wearing clothes that allowed them to easily hide weapons. When she'd portaled into the parking lot, she noticed those charged with watching over the external perimeter. All that was fine. It was adaptation to the world as it was, not surrender.

She didn't think there was any surrender in the Witches on Wheels, from the leader down to the newest probie. If there was, she hadn't seen any evidence of it.

Runeclaw jumped onto the bar before Scarlett got there, and Lin, who was tending, reached out to scratch the cat's ears. Runeclaw stretched his neck and pushed against her hand, and the drow shook her head with a laugh. "You're such a hedonist."

He countered, "I'm a cat."

Scarlett settled on one of the stools. "Pretty much the

same thing. He's either being a predator or lazing about reveling in luxury. Not much in between."

Runeclaw sneezed. "This would be a good moment to observe that you are particularly bad at providing appropriate luxury."

"Quit whining." Lin popped the top on a beer bottle and set it in front of Scarlett.

She sipped it. "Amber in yet?"

Lin shook her head. "Haven't seen her yet. She usually stops by for a bit even when she's working, so I imagine she'll be around eventually. You could message her."

"Nah. It's not important. I just wanted to know how her run went."

Lin departed to serve a couple of other people at the bar, then came back. "That seems important."

Runeclaw interjected, "Scarlett believes in ghosts."

She looked down at her partner. "You don't?"

"Projector, remember?"

"Projector for one of them. Not for the others."

Lin interjected, "What's all this, then?" Her fake English accent made them both laugh.

Scarlett replied, "When we were in Austin, we stayed at the Driskill Hotel."

Runeclaw interrupted, "Despite Scarlett promising we wouldn't go to any weird kitschy tourist spots."

"I promised we wouldn't go to any on the way. I didn't make any commitments about the destination itself. Now shut up." She turned her attention back to Lin.

"Anyway, the place is reputed to have ghosts, and we saw some. One was faked, for sure, which I guess I can't really fault the hotel for. Everyone's got to keep things interesting, right? But with the others we saw there was no sign of tech, and I had all of my magical senses active so I would have noticed if it was magic."

Scarlett shrugged. "There's more to life than this physical body, but I've never really thought about whether ghosts are real. I guess I still don't know. But the ones at the hotel seemed pretty real."

Lin nodded thoughtfully, then leaned on the bar on her forearms. "I've never seen a ghost, but I'm positive they exist. Sometimes people die, but their energy, their essence, doesn't fully dissipate. That's what ghosts are. Untethered energy."

Runeclaw asked, "So, they're stuck here before they can go on to the next phase?"

Lin shrugged. "Or they're gifted with more time here to deal with whatever keeps them around. I don't know. It's all conjecture."

Scarlett replied, "There's far more to the world than the part we see, that's for sure."

Amber slid into the seat next to her. "Are you talking about the dark web? Because that's a good description of the dark web."

Scarlett laughed. "No. Ghosts. Are there ghosts in the web?"

The infomancer put on a dramatic expression and voice. "We are all ghosts on the magical dark web, flitting about, hunting our enemies, unbound by that which previously housed us."

Lin snorted loudly and put a bottle in front of Amber. "Here you go. Ghost fuel."

Amber took a drink and sighed. "Perfect."

Scarlett was unable to wait. "So, how was your run?"

"Annoying as hell."

Runeclaw replied, "Why? Was Scarlett there?"

Scarlett grabbed a napkin off the bar and threw it at the cat. He swiped it out of the air, trapped it under a paw, and used another to slice it neatly in half. Scarlett raised an eyebrow. "Whoa, threatening."

Amber ignored them. "Robots. So many robots. In a bank. I hate banks."

Scarlett laughed. "I do too, after breaking into one with you."

Lin interjected, "Seconded."

Runeclaw added, "Thirded."

Amber scowled. "Shush."

She was silent until Scarlett asked, "So, are you gonna tell us, or are you just being a jerk?"

The other woman grinned. "The latter."

"I'll have Runeclaw claw you. So many times."

Amber raised her hands. "All right. I give up. So, the man we spotted is named Kingston Trane. He's old money. Lives in Nashville, Tennessee. This is only one of the companies he's involved with."

"And you think he's Veil?"

Amber shrugged. "He's bald, he's rich, and he's the only obvious tie between the facility and the organization. I think most of the signs point to yes."

Lin asked, "But you didn't find any other evidence against him?"

Amber shook her head. "The information I downloaded connected the company to the warehouse and him to the company. No obvious records of money moving around.

Technically, the warehouse is still in the company's possession, awaiting disposition during the bankruptcy hearings, which haven't been scheduled yet."

Scarlett tapped her fingers on the bar. "So, they're just basically, what, using it without permission?"

"Without any permission I could find in the system, anyway."

Lin *hmphed*. "The Veil certainly seems to be all over the place, doesn't it?"

Scarlett mused, "Boston, Provo, Austin, places in between. All over the country, anyway."

"How could something this wide-ranging stay secret for so long?"

Amber chuckled. "Magic. Both your kind and my kind. Get into the systems, erase the records, manipulate the databases. Plus, the same old stuff that companies have done all along to hide ownership interests and so forth by layering ownership through various companies. It's all about knowing the system and working it, I guess."

Scarlett blew out a breath. "Things were much simpler on Oriceran."

Runeclaw replied, "But far less interesting."

She looked at him. "Nicer people there."

He grinned. "More willing to let you pretend you're normal."

"Jerk."

"Cat."

Scarlett put a hand to her temple to rub her growing headache. "So, where do we stand?"

Amber shrugged. "We've got a solid lead on where to find one of the bastards. I'll get some Witches to do initial drone recon and get surveillance set up on his house."

Lin added, "We'll create a rotation to watch the feed in real-time so we don't miss anything."

Scarlett shook her head. It wasn't enough. "If they're using portals, we won't see anything. They'd be stupid to do anything important out in the open."

"So you're thinking we need to do some invasive surveillance, is that it?"

Runeclaw cautioned, "Dangerous."

Scarlett countered, "But necessary if we want to find out anything useful about him."

Amber shook her head. "This is a paranoid person with money. He's going to have sensors, guards, and all sorts of other fun things to prevent the sort of intrusion you're thinking of."

"I know. But I think we still need more than a drone and a couple of cameras."

"Well, if it turns out we need it, we'll do it. But let's start with the easy stuff first, okay?"

Scarlett gave in. "All right." She looked down at her phone, which had buzzed with a message. Her mood lifted a little, and it reflected in her voice. "Good news. They're going to let me talk to the woman we rescued tomorrow morning."

Lin asked, "What do you hope to achieve by talking to her?"

Scarlett stood, finished her drink, and set the empty on the bar. "Knocking one more chip in the wall that separates us from the Veil."

CHAPTER THIRTEEN

The next morning, Scarlett put on her normal outfit, then decided the leather jacket might be a bit much for a hospital. She left it behind, tucked her wand in her other boot, and met one of the Witches who portaled her to Boston.

From there, she took the subway to the hospital with Runeclaw riding on her shoulder as usual. They got some stares, but she had the impression that seeing a cat on the subway was not a notable occurrence for most of the other riders. This was a plus for the city, as far as she was concerned.

Once inside the hospital, she asked for directions at the reception desk. After providing them, the man said, "I'm sorry, pets aren't allowed in the hospital proper."

Scarlett crouched, and Runeclaw jumped onto a nearby table and laid down. Several children immediately came over to pat him, and Scarlett laughed as she rose. "I think he's in good hands."

The man smiled. "I'll keep an eye on him, too."

"Thanks. I won't be long." Scarlett took an elevator up to the fifth floor, then found the right door. Beyond it was an ordinary hospital room—white walls with equipment mounted on them, a couple of chairs for visitors, sterile and generally unwelcoming.

The woman she'd rescued was sitting upright in the bed, staring at a tablet. She looked up and greeted Scarlett with a smile. The former captive seemed healthy, although she had wires leading to sensors sticking out of the top of her hospital gown, and an IV ran into her arm from a trio of bottles that hung on a stand nearby.

Scarlett greeted, "Hi there."

"Hi. Thanks for coming. This place is totally boring."

Scarlett laughed and slid a stool to the side of the woman's bed. "I can imagine. You doing okay?"

"Yep. All good." She gestured at the IV and the equipment. "All this is for my lifelong medical issue. No biggie."

"But big enough that you had to wear a locator, which made all the difference for us."

The woman deadpanned, "So much luck, I can hardly believe it." They laughed together.

"I imagine you've answered questions already. I'm sorry to ask you to deal with more of them."

"I've had local, regional, and national level people in here, at least twice each. Nice ones, stern ones, and everything in between. One more round won't hurt me as long as you're not a jerk."

Scarlett laughed. "My cat says I am, but I'll try not to be. Can you tell me what you remember about the abduction?"

The woman closed her eyes as if picturing it. "I was walking down the street by myself. That's not unusual. Our campus is safe." She snorted. "Most of the time, anyway. I heard steps behind me but wasn't able to turn before a man was on each side of me, shoving their arms under mine and lifting me off the ground. I struggled, but the third man showed up and pointed a wand at me. My brain kind of went soft or something. I couldn't remember what I was doing or why I was doing it. That part's still hazy."

Scarlett nodded. "There are lots of confusion spells. They're impossible to defend against unless you're trained, or a more powerful magical."

The other woman adjusted her IV line, which had gotten tangled as she gestured. "Anyway, they carried me to a van that pulled up to the street and threw me in the back. Another man was inside waiting, and he stabbed me with a needle. Things after that are fuzzy."

"Do you remember what they looked like?"

The woman scowled. "Everyone has asked that, and I've tried really hard to remember, but their faces were strange. When I tried to concentrate on them, they changed, almost like liquid. Never the same image twice."

Scarlett replied, "Illusion magic. They prepared for this grab well."

"That's what the others said. They also thought the drug did something to block my memory of it all. So, that might be part of not being able to describe them, too."

Scarlett ran her fingers through her hair to hide her frustration. "They planned it well. I have to give that to them. Of course, they've had a lot of practice." She pushed down her anger. "How many others were with you?"

"I think one other captive was in the van when they threw me in. Eventually, when they were moving us around from place to place afterward, five of us were together. I'm not sure what happened to the others."

Scarlett hesitated. "But they treated you okay?"

The other woman gave a half smile. "Fine. They weren't even mean. Demanding, sure, but they could've treated us a lot worse. Well, me. I guess I don't know how they treated the others."

"Probably pretty well, since they'd want to avoid any damage. They're putting magical collars on the captives to diminish their will, then using them as servants. The ones we've seen all looked healthy. I can't say what's going on in their brains, of course, but there were no obvious signs of mistreatment."

The other woman's expression changed slightly as if that had lightened her concern. "I hope you're right."

Scarlett smiled. "Me too. Is there anything else you can remember that might help us?"

"I'm sorry. I really don't have anything. It's all too jumbled."

Scarlett rose and touched the other woman's hand. "You did good. Thanks."

A nurse came in. "You'll have to go now."

The woman on the bed added, "You better obey. They're tough around here."

They all shared a laugh, and Scarlett raised her hands. "I surrender. I'm gone."

She paused, grabbed the pad and pen at the side of the table, and scrawled on it. She handed it to the woman. "This is my phone number. If you need anything or remember anything else, please let me know." She stepped out of the room and stopped at the sight of two uniformed police officers, one blocking her path to the left and the other blocking her path to the right.

The one on the left asked, "Scarlett Prynne?"

She gave him a neutral nod. "That's me."

The other said, "We'd like you to come with us, please."

"Am I under arrest?"

The first one replied, "Not yet. All we know is that the lieutenant wants to talk to you."

Scarlett shrugged. "Sure. I'm happy to talk."

The second one smiled. "Maybe we'll arrest you afterward." His tone made it clear he was joking.

Scarlett chuckled. "Let's hope it doesn't come to that."

They escorted her down to the first floor and into a small office borrowed for the occasion. A man in a brown suit stood from behind the desk. He had nicely styled brown hair, slightly lighter than the suit, and black wire-rimmed glasses. He extended a hand. "I'm Detective Lieutenant James O'Shea."

She shook it. "Scarlett."

He nodded, gestured at the chair nearest her, then sat. "James. Thanks for agreeing to see me."

She looked over her shoulder at the police officer who stood inside the door. The other had remained outside. "There were threats of arrest."

The officer grinned. "Not threats. Not even veiled ones. Possibly suggestions."

O'Shea chuckled. "Well, whatever got the job done, I guess. So, my chief has been in touch with one Chief Stevenson in Provo."

Scarlett looked at him and winced. "Oh. That's not good."

O'Shea laughed. "Stephenson told my chief that you might be worried. But no, it is good. I'm here to answer questions. I understand you're after the jerks who kidnapped our college students."

Scarlett nodded. "I am. Were you able to get anything on the culprits?"

He shook his head with a scowl. "Nothing useful. We checked the cameras. I'm sure you did as well. There were signs that a whole bunch of infomancers accessed the information. The university's really going to have to upgrade its security, or its insurance company will have a fit." He waved that off. "Sorry. Anyway, no. They appear to have come in under an illusion, changed a couple of times while on campus, and used yet another to get away. We couldn't track them."

Scarlett shook her head. "It sucks having competent enemies."

"Especially when they have magic."

"True. Were you able to find anything that connected the people who were taken?"

He ran a hand through his hair in a way that seemed carefully practiced to avoid messing up the style. "Nothing connects the students to one another, and nothing connects any of them to the ones who've been taken before that Chief Stevenson provided to us. It seems truly random."

Scarlett exhaled an annoyed sigh. "That tracks with what we know. Still, it would've been nice if they'd screwed something up."

"Agreed."

"That's all I can think to ask. But if you give me your

card, I'll call with anything I think of later?" Her tone made it a question.

He handed over his card with a nod. "Absolutely. Can you give us anything to go on?"

"I wish I could. All I've got is the information that this is probably the last kidnapping spree if we're right about why they accelerated it. We think they moved all at once to gather what they needed because we've been pressuring them."

"To turn into servants or something?"

"That's what we think."

O'Shea rose. "Bastards."

Scarlett stood as well. "Absolute bastards."

"If you find anything, please share."

She shook his extended hand and was touched by his concern for the students who had been taken. "Count on it."

A few minutes later, she was out front of the hospital with Runeclaw. She shared what she'd discovered, and he observed, "Not much more than we had at the start of the day."

"Nope. And that's frustrating as hell."

"What now?"

She considered the question and couldn't think of any way to move the situation forward. Her mind was as blank as it had ever been. "I think we need a break from all this. Let's go see the Spell Riders."

CHAPTER FOURTEEN

Scarlett stepped onto the driveway in front of the Spell Riders' garage and took a moment to look at the place. Usually, she was in a hurry or so focused on her objective that she didn't take it in. The front of the building had eight separate garage doors, each leading to a work bay. The structure was at least twice as deep as the bays, maybe more. This suggested to Scarlett that it probably had been something before it was a garage, or perhaps she didn't understand the space requirements for an operation like this.

Six of the bays were occupied, with Spell Riders working on cars or motorcycles from the public, generating the cash flow that kept the organization running. The other two were for special projects, where the top mechanics, like Maddox, had their zones marked out.

The leader of the Spell Riders was hard at work in his area, the same one where he'd improved Dusk Runner for her. Shouts, playful insults, and the sounds of tools hammering, grinding, or whirring filled the air. Being around the controlled chaos always inspired a smile.

Scarlett made it behind Maddox without him becoming aware of her. He was using a powered tool to etch glyphs into the exhaust pipe of a motorcycle that was slightly bigger than Dusk Runner. The silver-on-silver designs were gorgeous. She asked, "What do those do?"

Maddox grinned at her. "Well, look what the cat dragged in." His gaze shifted to Runeclaw. "Thanks, cat."

Runeclaw snorted. "Don't mention it."

"They help keep down the noise of the exhaust. It's a pretty simple modification, but I only figured out how to do it really well recently. A lot of people are asking for it now."

"Are you the only one who knows how to do it?"

He grinned. "So far. Job security is a fine thing." He turned off the instrument, set it at his side, and rose to wrap her in a hug. "What can we do for you today?"

"I was hoping I could join you for lunch."

Maddox wiped his hands on a nearby rag. "Perfect. I was looking for an excuse to set this aside for a bit, anyway." He led her out into the area behind the garage. It was a wide swath of well-kept lawn, with an area for horseshoes and lawn darts on one side, several grills and coolers set up in various spots, and an assortment of mismatched lawn furniture.

He went first to a cooler. "Root beer, right?"

"Oh, yes, please." He laughed and handed her a bottle. She twisted off the top, took a long drink, and exhaled a happy sigh. "I needed that."

Maddox walked to a nearby grill, removed the lid and

the metal grate, and dumped a bunch of charcoal into it. He used his wand to start it burning, then covered it again. He sat on a lounge chair, leaned back, and closed his eyes. "That'll be ready to go in about thirty minutes. Until then, why don't you tell me what you've been up to."

"I spent the morning with the girl we rescued from the Luminous Veil."

"How is she?"

"She's good."

"Did she have any useful information to share?"

Scarlett let out an "Oof" as Runeclaw jumped onto her stomach, then laid on top of her, stretching out and closing his eyes. She patted him on the head. "Basically nothing. They used illusion to disguise themselves. I scored a contact with the local police, though, so that's something. He confirmed there's no obvious connection among the captives."

Maddox grunted. "Good that the girl's okay, unfortunate that there's nothing to go on."

"Well, we did make some recent progress along another line of inquiry. We found a facility set up to make those collars and have it under surveillance."

Maddox opened one eye and gave her a dour look. "And you didn't lead with that? You're just mentioning it now?"

Scarlett chuckled. "I wanted to keep your expectations low. Build up to it."

Runeclaw murmured, "Don't try to be clever. You're not good at it."

Maddox added with a playful growl, "What he said. So, what's the plan?"

Scarlett replied, "We wait for something to happen,

then we go in and slap some people around. Ideally, we slap them so hard that all their secrets fall out."

"Do you need us?"

"I'm not in charge anymore, you know that. Wren is the decision-maker. She will or she won't, based on whatever arcane metrics she uses to make decisions. No one I've talked to seems to know why she does what she does in any particular situation."

Maddox laughed. "More likely than not she won't ask for backup unless you're facing double opposition. She's competitive."

"With you?"

He waved negligently. "With me. With everyone. But definitely with the bad guys. She doesn't just want to beat them. She wants to grind them into the dust and humiliate them too."

Scarlett nodded. That sounded like Wren. "Can't say I argue with that approach."

"Nor I. I think in her case it's because she grew up with brothers. That constant competitiveness might come from there. Whatever it is, it serves her and the Witches well."

Scarlett took a sip of soda. "I feel kind of bad that I got them and you mixed up in this."

Maddox slashed a hand in her direction. "Don't. We do what we want, when we want. It's why the organizations exist. If we didn't think this was valuable, we'd do something else."

Scarlett had to admit, she didn't see a way to make either organization do something they didn't want to do. "Okay. So, tell me something entertaining to balance out all this waiting."

Maddox laughed. "Entertaining?" He sat up on his chair and lifted a hand to shade his eyes as he looked at her. "Okay, let me tell you the story of Snow and the lawn darts."

Scarlett grinned. "This has to be good."

"Depends on who you're asking, I suppose. Anyway, we were having one of our big cookouts. People all over the place, lots of food and drink, a generally good time. We had a lawn dart tournament going. You know, the kind with brackets, where people play one match, the winner goes on to face the winner of another match, and so on. Snow is good at lawn darts, but he's far from the best. He wasn't likely to win outright, and everyone knew it. So, he got it into his head to cheat a little."

"Is that frowned upon?"

Maddox shrugged. "Not if it's done with style. Basically, the house rule is anything you get away with is okay."

"That seems like a quick route to trouble."

Maddox laughed. "Often. So, anyway, he modified the lawn darts. Added little airfoils and a tiny engine. I'm not sure if he remote-controlled them or if they had some sort of artificial intelligence in them, and he's never said."

"I'm guessing they didn't work exactly as he'd hoped."

Maddox scratched his beard. "The first two worked perfectly. He tossed them, and they landed almost dead center in the ring. The thing is, those were both pretty good throws already, so they didn't need much adjustment."

Scarlett could picture Snow being smug after the first two throws, maybe even grandstanding a bit. "And then?"

"Then Snow decided to get clever. He threw the third

one up high, where it would require far more adjustment to land in the right spot. I don't know why he did it, and he won't answer that question, either. But when the dart tried to make its adjustment, it misfired."

Scarlett smothered a laugh. "Oh no."

Maddox nodded. "Oh yes. So, we have this pointy little rocket flying out of control. Witches and wizards were diving out of the way of the thing as it whipped through the area. Others managed shields, which only deflected the dart onto new paths and created more chaos."

Scarlett was trying to control her laughter but not doing a very good job of it. "That must've been quite a scene."

"Not nearly as impressive as when it hit a propane tank and exploded."

"Oh no."

Maddox slapped his hands together. "Oh yes. I'm sure you've noticed that some of these heathens use propane grills instead of charcoal. Well, fortunately, people had gotten shields around everyone and everything, so the damage was minimal when it went up. But now Snow is banned from all games involving edges or points. And we keep a wary eye on him when he plays horseshoes."

Scarlett laughed again. "That seems wise." Maddox shared a couple more stories about Snow, then Scarlett asked, "How did he meet Diana and her team?"

"He had some talent in an area of magic or technology they needed to know about. Probably magic since they're awful sharp on technology already."

She nodded. "I got a look at it when I visited. Sure would like to play in their toy box."

Maddox laughed. "Me too. But beyond that, Snow won't talk about it."

"A real man of mystery, our Snow."

"For sure."

The conversation turned to other things, and Scarlett enjoyed sharing lunch and conversation with Maddox and a number of the other riders who came out to join them. When she and Runeclaw had eaten their fill, she looked at her phone and sighed. "It's my turn on facility surveillance in an hour, so I better get going."

Maddox hugged her. "We're here when you need us."

"I know. Thanks." She grinned. "Try to keep Snow out of trouble, won't you?"

The leader of the Spell Riders rolled his eyes. "Far easier said than done, I'm afraid, but I'll do my best. Runeclaw, you try to keep her out of trouble."

The cat snorted. "Impossible. Have you met her?"

CHAPTER FIFTEEN

Scarlett and Runeclaw walked through the front door of Wheels together and discovered the place was mostly full of locals, with only a few of the expected Witches standing guard. Scarlett vectored toward Lin, who was behind the bar and talking to a pair of Witches.

The drow noticed her approach and pointed across the room. Scarlett's gaze followed the path and spotted Amber at the end of it. She walked over and plopped into the booth across from the infomancer. "What's going on?"

"Something's happening at the facility." Amber tapped on her keyboard and gestured, and a holographic image appeared above it.

Runeclaw had jumped on the table. He batted at it, which started it spinning slowly.

"There are some guards on the ground and at least one more up on the roof. You can barely see him from this view, but the overhead drone shows him clearly."

Scarlett asked, "Where is this coming from?"

"We placed a couple of cameras nearby."

"Do we think something important is happening?"

"We've got more people on the inside, too, according to thermals. Wren thinks it's enough to move on."

Lin arrived. "So let's get moving, slacker."

They portaled together to the warehouse and headed for the lockers. Scarlett opened hers, took off her leather jacket, and tossed it on a nearby bench. "Are we going in right away?"

Lin shrugged as she changed into the black trousers and T-shirt that served the Witches as a base layer. "Don't think so. Wren just said to get ready. When she uses that particular tone, we don't ask questions. We just do what she says."

"Gotcha." Scarlett changed out of her jeans and T-shirt into the matching base layer, then put her boots on and shoved her backup wand into the right one. At this point, it was more a good luck talisman than something she thought she'd need. Still, she probably would've said the same thing when she'd gotten kicked through the portal and lost her main wand, so having it was good backup.

She reached into her locker and pulled out the bulletproof vest. She scowled at it but put it on without complaint.

As she twisted and turned to check the fit, Lin commented, "Good. You can learn. Runeclaw said you couldn't, but I had hoped you'd eventually realize you needed to wear the vest without whining about it all the time."

"I don't like either of you."

They both laughed.

Scarlett redid one of the straps to make sure it was as

tight as possible, then slid on the harness that would hold Fang in its place against her ribs. Next up, her knives went onto her back, and her wrist sheaths holding her throwing daggers slid into place on her arms. She looked over as Lin put the small crossbow Scarlett had bought her into a leather and fabric sheath on her right thigh. "You figured out how to carry it. Nice."

"Took some custom work, but it's good now. Stays in place. Not heavy at all. And it's good to have the nonlethal option at hand." Lin frowned. "Although I don't think we'll be trying anything so gentle today."

Scarlett nodded. "Yeah. Good point." She drew the revolver from its holster at the small of her back and emptied the chambers, then loaded in five anti-magic rounds. Since this was their best chance to take out the members of the Luminous Veil before they got done with whatever they were planning, they wouldn't be pulling any punches. She put the pistol back where it belonged, then strapped the bandolier of tranquilizer darts over the vest. Their ability to pierce tight magical shields might come in handy.

Finally, she slipped her jacket on, checked to ensure her wand was where it belonged in the sleeve, and rolled her shoulders. "I feel like some kind of a soldier in this thing."

Lin laughed. "It's good to hear you say that since you'll be carrying a rifle, too."

Scarlett put a note of whining into her voice. "But Mom."

"Shut it. Wren's orders. Even if you empty the magazine and throw it away, you're taking it."

"Fine."

Runeclaw snarked, "I guess you're right. She can learn."

Before Scarlett could counter the insult, Wren appeared in the room alongside several other Witches who headed straight for their lockers.

Wren announced, "The plan is to surround the place. We'll get moving as soon as we can, and everyone can join when they're ready. Amber doesn't anticipate any immediate action based on the number of people inside and our guess about the process of making the collars. We should have the time we need to get into position."

Lin called, "Are the Spell Riders coming along?"

"They'll be nearby as a reserve and will catch anyone trying to flee. But we're not gonna need them. Because the Witches are going to stomp these Luminous Veil scumbags' heads in."

A round of cheers went up, and Wren pointed at Scarlett and Lin. "You two, take Ella with you and find a good staging area near the building. She can stay and get the rest of us there while you two move into position."

Lin handed a rifle to Scarlett, which she clipped on with its sling around her neck. They moved to one side of the room and portaled to the industrial park that held the Luminous Veil's facility.

Leaving Ella to handle transporting the rest of their allies, Scarlett, Lin, and Runeclaw moved under a veil through the grassy areas outside a pair of other facilities before arriving near their target.

Amber spoke into their ears over the comm. "All right. They've got more guards in static locations than before. I think there are cars driving around watching over the place, too. What do you see?"

Lin replied, "Confirmation on the cars and the increased number of guards outside. They're all wearing jackets or baggy clothing that might be hiding rifles or at least pistols. There's one on each corner on the part of the roof we can see."

"That matches what I see. We've got a handful more on the inside. If I had to guess, they're getting ready for something that'll be happening before too long."

Wren instructed, "Scarlett, Lin, move around the right side of the building. Let's get a sense of what they've got over there. Look for natural features to hide behind since there's no telling what sensors they might have running."

Amber reported, "I don't know if they've got magic detection running, but I'm only seeing signals coming out a short distance from the building." Those areas were illuminated in their display glasses as blotches of color on the aerial map view.

Scarlett replied, "Once they get started, they'll probably have to deactivate any magic detection. I'm sure the collar-making process involves a lot of magic."

"I'm sure you're right."

Scarlett and Lin crept along the side. Lin observed, "Got another guard at the far corner on the roof."

Another Witch, presumably on the other side of the arrangement, announced, "One over here, too."

A van pulled up near the front of the building.

"Wait one. Something's happening." A moment later, Lin continued. "New arrivals. Looks like eight. They're dressed like soldiers. Body armor. Rifles. Pretty sure I see grenades on their belts."

Wren replied, "So, that tells us something interesting is

imminent. Good. Everyone, find some concealment, just in case they deploy more sensors."

Scarlett and Lin found a nearby electrical box they could hide behind.

Wren asked, "Amber, can you see inside?"

"No. The skylights are angled, and I can't get a good view from where I am. The only way to do it would be to bring the drone down, and they'd probably notice that."

Runeclaw offered, "I could go up and look. They might not react to a cat. All you have to do is get the portal hidden well enough they don't notice."

Scarlett cautioned, "I don't think that's such a good idea," but repeated the idea to Wren.

Wren instructed, "Hold off. Might need to use it, though, so figure out the right location for your portal."

A few moments later, Amber reported, "Just got ten more thermal signatures inside, near where the equipment is, and another half-dozen in other places. Looks like they came through several portals rather than one, based on how they appeared."

Scarlett observed, "All the bald baddies coming out to play."

Wren replied, "Perfect. We'll give them ten minutes to get into it. Then we'll strike. Amber, start the countdown."

CHAPTER SIXTEEN

Amber counted down from twenty, giving everyone time to prepare. Scarlett patted her chest. Runeclaw jumped up and sank his claws into her armored vest. She cradled him against the rifle Lin had insisted she carry and drew her wand with her other hand. "Once we're up top, move to my shoulder so I can shoot."

"Got it."

Scarlett appreciated that his attitude showed he was totally focused on the mission ahead, ready to bring some havoc down on the Luminous Veil. Lin's face showed she was as well, which made three of them. When Amber hit zero, Scarlett and Lin launched skyward on blasts of force magic.

Their position was toward the center of the roof, which meant they were between the guards at the corners. Team Three was already flying into view to their right to deal with the guards nearest them. Scarlett hit the surface running, and Runeclaw scrambled up to free her hands.

She gripped the rifle, pointed it roughly toward the

skylight, and held the trigger down. Bullets slammed into the glass and sent shards raining down into the building as the barrage created an opening. She hit the button to release the rifle's strap and tossed the weapon away as she ran. Her pistol was in her hand as she jumped through the skylight.

Time slowed as she plummeted, movement coming in flashes as people reacted below and shocked faces looked up, fingers pointing out the intruder in their midst. Molten metal flowed from the furnaces at the end of the channels to gather in the center crucible where they formed the collars.

The thought that if she'd been unlucky, her flight might have landed her in that wickedly hot material flitted across her mind as she calculated her landing point. Fortunately, it was between the channels.

Runeclaw's nails dug into her shirt outside the protection of her armored vest as he repositioned in preparation for the fight ahead. She landed with a burst of force magic to cushion the impact and fell into a roll as her partner jumped away. When she came up, she pointed her revolver at the nearest bald man in glimmering robes and pulled the trigger.

The anti-magic round crossed the distance between them in an instant. It would've removed his head from his body and thus him from the fight if a man dressed in a black suit hadn't leapt in front of him. The bullet struck the man in the chest, but no blood appeared. Scarlett growled, "Some kind of body armor." She tried another shot, but the robed figure was already in motion, diving for protection behind part of the collar-making equipment that lay between her and him.

She swung the gun to her right in search of another target but held her fire as the ground-level doors broke open and the Witches flowed in. She couldn't risk a shot under that circumstance for fear it might hit an ally. She shoved the gun into its holster and shouted to Runeclaw, "Good hunting."

Runeclaw moved beneath the channels of molten metal suspended in the stone above, using the limited shadows it provided as cover. Bullets flew around him, people filled the air with screams, and magic spewed out back and forth as both sides did their best to eliminate the other. He ignored the surrounding chaos except when it became necessary to dodge or redirect. He was after the big prey.

When a body-armored man appeared between the channels in front of him, Runeclaw blasted him with lightning from his tail. The man shivered and stuttered as his eyes rolled up in his head, and Runeclaw jumped over him as he continued forward.

When the next man was thrown underneath the channel, Runeclaw dashed to the side to avoid him and took cover behind the central receptacle for all of that molten metal. The heat coming off it was extraordinary, but he needed its protection while he assessed the battle, so he'd have to endure it.

Several enemies were in positions he could reach in relative safety, but he resisted the urge to engage. His reservoir of magic was deep but not limitless, and he didn't want to waste it on unimportant targets. He spotted robes swishing on the floor nearby as one of the bald baddies repositioned.

Runeclaw dashed out to engage, but a soldier chose that moment to step in the way. Runeclaw jumped onto the man's shoulder, whipped his tail around, touched the man's nose, and blasted him with lightning.

His gaze snapped up at the sound of a female scream, and he spotted the bald baddie in turquoise robes hammering a Witch with his magic. She was on the floor, bleeding from the leg, and had both hands up as if to ward him off. The one holding a wand was barely maintaining a shield against his attack. It flickered and compressed inward as Runeclaw watched, then fell away completely.

Before the bald baddie could loose his kill shot, Runeclaw leapt from the falling soldier's shoulder onto that of the man in the turquoise robes. He reached around and raked his extended claws across the man's eyes. The bald man screamed in anger, and his wand flicked upward to point at Runeclaw.

The sizzle of shadow magic shot past him as he leapt from the man's shoulder to his head. Another swipe of his claws opened the man's forehead to dump blood into his eyes, and Runeclaw jumped away again as another blast of magic, further off target, sought him.

When he landed on the man's other shoulder, he stretched and raked his front claws across the man's neck. Blood spurted, but not as much as there should've been if Runeclaw had hit something important.

He jumped off as the man fell and landed lightly before

the bald baddie thumped beside him. With an expression of complete disdain, Runeclaw blasted the man with lightning to ensure he would stay down. Then he went to watch over the wounded Witch as she struggled to regain her focus.

Scarlett had calculated that her best role in this particular fight was to winnow out the fighters. Other Witches' skills equaled hers at magic-to-magic combat, but she had the edge over most when it came to being in the center of the battle.

Her first move had been to engage one of the bald baddies' assistants, a frightened-looking man in a suit who had conquered his fear enough to produce a pistol from somewhere and fire it at her. He missed as she sidestepped and ducked, and Scarlett flicked her wand to rip the gun out of his hand.

A look of shock filled his face as he realized he was defenseless. It changed to one of pain as she surged forward and stabbed him in the thigh with Fang. She twisted the knife as she pulled it out, guaranteeing a larger wound that would keep him down even if he woke up from the tranquilizing poison that was now inside him.

Her head snapped around at a woman's scream, and she saw one of her allies falling backward with one hand pressed to a bleeding shoulder. An enemy stood a dozen feet away with his rifle tracking downward to shoot her again.

Reflex took over, and Scarlett threw Fang at the soldier.

The dagger tumbled as it flew through the air. She held her breath, hoping she'd thrown it well enough to stop his finger from tightening on the trigger. The blade sank into the man's neck and the gun dropped, forgotten, as he reached up to the wound, then swayed and collapsed.

Scarlett waved her wand, and Fang flew back to her hand, dripping a trail of blood. She shoved the dagger into its sheath, grabbed a throwing knife, and hurled it at a bald baddie who was too far away for her to make the throw with Fang.

The knife flew true, but the man's reflexes were fast. It missed his head by an inch and clanged off one of the hoppers full of ore. She cursed and made a mental note of its location in the hope that she could retrieve it later.

Scarlett drew Fang again, and a surge of energy flowed into her accompanied by the palpable sensation of the dagger's pleasure at the fight. She charged toward another of the suited figures and leapt over one of the channels of molten metal. A blast of force magic struck her in midair and knocked her off target despite the shields that protected her from damage. She stumbled as she landed, then angled in pursuit of the fleeing man.

Her target ran past a soldier engaged with a Witch, and Scarlett couldn't resist the opportunity. She threw herself to the floor in a slide and slashed Fang across the back of the man's calves. The magical dagger penetrated the shield that someone had put on him without slowing, and the man went down with a scream. She transitioned back up to her feet without slowing and kept running, then hurled Fang at the man and missed.

Fortunately, he had run near one of the hoppers of

metal. Scarlett twitched her wand to lift a piece of ore out of the top, then slashed it down to throw the ore at the man's head. The man flew forward to land bonelessly on the floor and slid a few feet on his face.

Scarlett brought Fang back to her hand as motion from the side caught her eye, and she twisted to see a portal opening. She dodged behind the stone channel of molten metal as a soldier appeared and a rifle opened up on her. The bullets passed unaffected through her magical shield. She snarled, "Reinforcements. Elite soldiers. Anti-magic ammunition. Watch out."

CHAPTER SEVENTEEN

Scarlett grabbed the grenades Lin had shoved into her pockets before they left the warehouse, primed them, and hurled them at the new arrivals. A magical must have been watching the newcomers because her projectiles flew up in different directions before they went off, wasting the high-voltage stun charge inside them. She muttered a string of curses as she navigated through other fights toward the soldiers, occasionally getting close enough to lash out with one of her knives or deliver a punch to assist her allies.

Wren snapped over the comm, "Guard."

Scarlett turned her attention entirely to defense. She layered shields on herself and Runeclaw, who was halfway across the room from her but easily targeted through her magic connection to his pendant. Then she threw more around every ally in sight. She spotted the group of four men in robes clustered together in a corner an instant before the entire warehouse turned cold.

Icicles grew on every surface, even the hot stone of the

metal channels, then broke off and darted around the room. More appeared with each passing second to add to the blizzard of frozen needles.

Scarlett threw a blast of force magic at the foursome, but it bounced ineffectually off their protective shields. Each time an icicle hit her shields, it pulled at her power and weakened her defenses, which wouldn't last forever given how many people she was protecting. She focused on her inner reservoir of magic and set her mind to pumping more energy into shields, but she didn't see a way out of the sudden and unexpected stalemate.

The situation worsened as gunshots sounded at a rate that made her think of buzzing bees. The other Witches wouldn't risk hitting their allies unless one of them had a perfect shot, and this barrage wasn't focused enough for that. A scream signaled that someone had been hit. Scarlett ground her teeth together as she readied herself to rush the foursome, figuring it wouldn't be worse than waiting to be shot.

Then Wren snapped, "Amber."

"On it."

A moment later, an unbroken skylight above shattered, and a dark object whipped through it. Scarlett's mind registered the shape as a drone as it reached the foursome of bald men in robes, crashed onto the floor beside them, and exploded. Their shields protected them enough to keep them upright, but the blizzard stopped.

Scarlett snapped, "Runeclaw, Gold Robes."

Runeclaw's elation at no longer being pinned down by the blizzard of icicles matched his joy at having been given a target. Gold Robes wasn't among the four who had been casting the hostile magic, and it took Runeclaw a moment to locate him. He was on the far side of the room, about thirty feet away, crouched in the shelter of one of the hoppers.

Runeclaw realized the man was probably the one who had defended the foursome as they cast the blizzard spell. He dashed forward and felt Scarlett move at the same moment. She was visible in the corner of his eye as they raced toward the same spot.

A man reared up in front of him, frantically pulling a pistol down to aim. Runeclaw laughed inwardly at the expression on the man's face, which suggested he didn't start the day expecting he'd be trying to shoot a cat before it was over.

A blast of lightning from his tail dropped the man, and his shot slammed into one of the stone channels. A drip of molten metal fell into Runeclaw's path, and he threw himself to the side to avoid it, which also helped him evade the next couple of bullets someone sent in his direction. When he looked up at the man who had shot at him, the soldier was falling to the floor with a throwing knife sticking out of the junction between shoulder and neck.

Runeclaw sent a wave of approval through his connection to Scarlett and dashed through the legs of three different fights between Witches and the elite soldiers. He blasted one of them but wanted to keep his energy up for when he met Gold Robes. Finally, after leaping over the body of another falling man who had one of Scarlett's darts protruding from his forehead, he was close enough.

Runeclaw leapt up at the bald baddie, who stumbled backward in the face of the unexpected attack. The man had a force shield tight against his skin, but Runeclaw's nails sank through it into the middle of his chest. He reached up and stabbed them in a little higher, climbing and scratching the man at the same time. He'd made it almost to the man's neck when a wave of force lifted him and threw him away without warning.

He careened through the air and spread his paws wide to control his trajectory. With a stab of fear, he realized he was heading right for one of the channels. He screamed for Scarlett, but a moment later, Lin came into view, jumped over the channel, and caught him before he landed in it. She crushed him against her body armor. "I've got you, buddy."

Unfortunately, Gold Robes had tracked his flight, and from the man's expression as he stared into Runeclaw's eyes, he wasn't pleased with the cat's attack. He lifted his wand to deliver some payback.

Scarlett had been thrown off her stride by Runeclaw's danger, but once she'd seen Lin running toward him, she had trusted her friend to save her partner. Her attention returned to the man in the Gold Robes as he lifted his wand. She couldn't reach him in time, and his magic would doubtless protect him from hers long enough to get his attack off. She pulled Fang back, focused on the shoulder of the arm that held Gold Robes' wand, and hurled the dagger.

Fang tumbled end over end, as always seeming to move in slow motion as she watched, then struck and sank in almost to the hilt. Anger rippled through Scarlett as she watched Gold Robes clutch the dagger in his throat and go down. She couldn't believe she had missed so badly, especially since she'd wanted to take him prisoner and beat every last scrap of information out of him.

She used her wand to pull the dagger back to her, and as soon as it reached her hand, she whipped it in an arc at the soldier coming in from her right. He leaned back to avoid it and delivered a kick to her side that knocked her backward. She wondered why he hadn't shot. Then the soldier she hadn't spotted on the other side of her threw an elbow at her head. Her peripheral vision caught it just in time for her to drop and avoid it.

When she hit the floor on her back, she lifted her knees to her chest, wrenched her body to the side, and delivered a kick to the closest one's knee. The joint bent the wrong way with a disturbing *crunch*, followed by his scream as he fell. Scarlett popped back up to whip the pistol the other one had drawn out of his hand with her wand hand.

She stabbed him with Fang, but the dagger glanced off his body armor and failed to penetrate. Her force shield mostly deflected his punch to her face and barely moved her head. She tried another attack with the dagger again, but he blocked it and rammed his body into hers in an attempt to knock her over.

Scarlett set her feet and pushed back, but he went down suddenly, and she overbalanced. His foot landed hard against her blocking arm when they were both on the floor, and he pulled a nasty serrated knife from his boot.

She pointed her wand at him and spoke a command. A force blast sent him and his weapon sliding across the room, far out of melee range. She winced a silent apology at the Witch the sliding man had knocked down, then forced herself back to her feet. She was up for only a moment before bullets slammed into both of her legs and dropped her to the floor. Pain made her scream as she dragged herself behind the nearest cover. Runeclaw arrived beside her as she popped the top off her healing potion, and he guarded her as she drank it.

A moment later, she was ready to reenter the fight. Wren's voice came over the comm. "The baddies are retreating."

Scarlett growled, "Don't let them get away." She pulled her pistol and searched for a target. Gold Robes had been away from the other baddies. The four remaining robed men were near each other. She picked one and fired at him.

A soldier rushing to follow the quartet took the round in the back and kept running. His armor had protected him from the bullet. A moment later, the bald baddies portaled away.

The remaining soldiers, assistants, and guards made a concerted effort to run for the exits, but without their magical support, the Witches quickly subdued them. Scarlett, Wren, Lin, and Runeclaw met in the center of the room. Scarlett complained, "Bastards got away. Again."

Lin replied, "Yeah, they suck."

Runeclaw suggested, "Understatement."

A sudden explosion from the corner of the room

eclipsed Wren's reply. Wren snapped, "Out, immediate." That was the absolute command to flee.

Scarlett and Lin opened portals and jumped through, as did the rest of the Witches. They landed in a field a short distance from the warehouse and snapped their portals closed as fire and noise came from the other side.

Amber growled, "Report."

Everyone said their name, one by one, in the particular order that was standard for their operations. Scarlett's stress lessened with each new name, and she blew out a breath as the count finished and revealed they hadn't lost anyone.

Amber announced, "The place is gone. Blew up. It's just rubble."

Scarlett snarled, "Damn it. Again, they cut us off from any clues."

Wren wiped sweat and dirt from her forehead. "We've hurt them. That's enough for tonight. It's a win."

Scarlett nodded and didn't reply. To her, it felt like a loss and the chopping off of one more thread that might have led them to wherever the Veil operated from.

CHAPTER EIGHTEEN

Camus sat at his comfortable wooden desk with his fountain pen in hand and inscribed his latest notes in his daily journal. He updated it two or three times a day, spilling out the most important things onto paper for his later review and for the edification of the leaders who would follow him.

Those who had gone before him had not been quite so thorough, but the process helped him keep things straight. It also allowed him to eject things from his mind that he didn't need to hold onto, confident they would be waiting in the pages when he reviewed them in the days and weeks to come.

He was interrupted as Ellis barged into the room after only a quick knock to signal a visitor, not even waiting to be granted permission. The other man was disheveled, his hair sticking up in several directions, his body armor and tactical clothing stained with blood and dust. It was rare for him to see his subordinate in what Ellis referred to as his "work clothes." Something untoward had happened to bring him here like that.

Camus closed the ledger and cleared his mind. "What?"

Ellis seemed injured or maybe exhausted. His back was no longer the ramrod straight pole it usually was, but his voice was strong. "The witch and her friends hit the collar-making ritual. I don't know how they found it." Anger was evident in his tone. Camus wasn't sure he'd ever seen the other man this visibly upset.

"And?"

"Gold Robes is dead."

Camus scowled. That was one of the two he knew to be loyal. "Of course it would be one I could trust. And the facility?"

A trace of uncertainty passed across Ellis' face. "Lost. I destroyed it once it was clear we had no chance of defeating the witch and her friends. Hopefully I caught a few of them in the destruction."

"I doubt our luck is so good that you've removed the witch from the table, but your choice was a good one. It's what I would've ordered had there been time for you to ask." He pointed at the chair across the desk from him. "Sit before you fall."

As Ellis moved to obey, Camus pressed a button and quietly ordered sparkling water and whiskey for two. They sat in silence until the servant came in with the tray and left it on the desk.

Camus poured whiskey for Ellis and handed it over, then the same for himself, mixing it with a little sparkling water. As he sipped, he kept a subtle watch on the other man. When it seemed as if Ellis had recaptured his balance, Camus requested, "Explain more."

Ellis drew a deep breath. "I was positioned in the corner, away from the equipment. I didn't want the commands I was giving to interfere with the process or vice versa."

Camus nodded. "Wise."

"Things got underway without any problem. Then, suddenly, it all broke into chaos. The bastards had surrounded the building and came in from all directions almost simultaneously. The first ones arrived from above, plunging through the skylights. It threw the robes and the guards into immediate confusion.

"My people began to fight them off, and we brought more in by portal as the battle went on. The robes fought well, but something came in from above and exploded on them. Their shields protected them, but it turned the tide of the fight. I saw Gold Robes go down with a knife in the throat."

Ellis swallowed hard, and Camus interjected, "What we do is risky. He knew that. We all do."

Ellis nodded and dug for the strength to keep speaking. "Once most of my people and all the robes were out, I ran through the portal last and detonated the charges. I have a drone headed in that direction to see the result, but I doubt it will provide any useful information."

Camus sipped his whiskey and resisted the urge to sigh in frustration. The fact of the attack was more annoying to him than the results. "How do you think they found it?"

Ellis only half-suppressed a snarl. "I have no idea.

Maybe they tracked one of the guards. Maybe it was dumb luck. Maybe one of the robes did something." He shook his head. "The only thing I'm confident of is that it wasn't my people. The attackers had to have been in place before we got there."

Camus nodded. "Still. Anyone who will be present at the gathering, double- and triple-check everything about them. If you have any doubt, any at all, pay them a bonus not to attend. Send them away."

He thought about that for a second, then amended, "No, have them act normally. Even sending them away might give a watching enemy a clue. But assign them tasks other than the gathering."

"It will be done. Do you want us to counterattack their bar?" Ellis' tone made it clear he hoped the answer would be yes.

Camus considered it carefully. It would be rewarding, and the risk wasn't too great. He could always get more soldiers.

"No. Let them think they've won. We have no reason to go public again. From here on out, we stay in the shadows. Nothing they've discovered should have given them a clue about the gathering's existence or location, and everything else we have to do will be done in secret."

Ellis nodded, then drew a deep breath to steady himself. "The process was interrupted. We don't have enough collars."

"I know." Camus took another sip of his whiskey. "Select the best candidates for the collars we have. The others…" He considered his options. "Wipe their memories and set them free."

Ellis blinked. "Are you sure?"

Camus waved the question away and leaned back in his chair. "Far from any of our operations, of course, but yes. Given our run of unexpectedly bad luck, I hesitate to think what the result of killing them might be."

"You could send them to the World In Between." The words sounded reluctant.

"I reserve that fate only for my worst enemies. These do not qualify. So, we'll let them live." He thought for a second, then added, "Also, inform the others that each will have to give up one servant to be reassigned at the gathering. I will need them several days beforehand to examine their collars to ensure they are still functioning properly."

Ellis offered a half smile. "To ensure the others haven't manipulated the collars."

"Exactly."

"I'll see to it." The other man rose and departed at Camus' nod of permission.

Camus leaned back in his chair and closed his eyes. *Damn that witch. When this is done, I will see her and all her friends destroyed. They are most worthy of banishment to the World In Between once we've delivered enough pain to them.*

But first, we focus on achieving our plans. The gathering. Then, the elimination of those who can't be trusted. After that, we spread our influence wide and make our new puppets dance to our tune. Then, and only then, I will focus everything I am on the witch's destruction.

Ellis immediately headed to the security area, where his subordinates were waiting. He noticed one of them was missing. "Where is Franklin?"

One of the others said, "He didn't make it out of the warehouse."

Ellis pinched the bridge of his nose and muttered, "Damn that witch. No time to mourn now. We need to do several things right the hell now. First, we need to vet everyone who will be at the gathering."

"We've done that."

"I know. Do it again. Then do it a third time."

The woman in charge of the security at the gathering nodded. "Consider it done."

Ellis said, "I need meetings set up with each of the surviving robes so I can tell them they're losing a servant."

One of the others chuckled. "I'll take care of it. They won't like that."

Ellis winced at the thought of how much they wouldn't like it. "No. They definitely will not. Hopefully they'll take it out on Camus rather than me. He can handle it. Hell, he'll probably welcome it."

They discussed a few more things, and he sent them off to do their work. He took the woman in charge of the gathering aside. "We need even more security during the event. I have a very bad feeling about the witch and her friends."

She frowned. "I'm not sure I can do more without making it visible."

"I understand. Keeping it subtle is of utmost importance. Do every single thing you can think of within those bounds. And stage people on the grounds, hidden. At least they'll be close if something does go down."

She nodded and headed off. Ellis headed for the shower and a well-deserved rest. Only two more obstacles remained, the collaring ritual and the gathering. Surely, they could get through those without any additional interference. As he drifted off to sleep with that thought in his mind, he thought he heard mocking laughter.

CHAPTER NINETEEN

Wheels was full of tired Witches, plus several locals who were engaged in quiet conversations at the bar. The latter were experienced enough with the way the Witches on Wheels worked to know it was a time for calm and relaxation.

Scarlett, Lin, Wren, and Amber were seated at a round table with Runeclaw lying on top of it. Pizza boxes sat in the middle, and the remains of pizza slices in front of each of them, mainly crumbs, although for some reason Amber didn't eat the crust of her pizza. From Scarlett's angle, it looked like Runeclaw had his eye on that crust and would probably make a move to steal it before too long.

They'd all showered after the fight, then spent some time doing whatever they each needed to recover before meeting for dinner. Scarlett felt rumpled, even though she wore her favorite jeans and T-shirt. The others looked like they felt the same. She was also annoyed, and the others mirrored that emotion. Except for Runeclaw, who had stretched out on his side, made himself as long as possible, and feigned sleep while he kept a wary eye on Amber's plate.

Lin grumbled, "It was a damn good backup plan."

Amber replied, "Can't argue with that."

"Wonder how many of their own they took out."

Wren replied, "The bald baddies were all clear, from what I saw. Just helpers and soldiers left."

Scarlett snorted. "So, no one important."

"I'm sure that's how they felt about it at the time."

"I hate these guys."

The others at the table agreed, and Amber added, "This has to have hurt them, though. In a big way. Those collars must be pivotal to whatever their long-term plans are. They wouldn't go through all of this just to have servants, would they?"

Scarlett grumbled, "Agreed. But we're no closer to knowing what that might be than before we went after the facility." She took a deep swallow from her bottle of beer. "Damn, I'd really hoped this would lead somewhere."

Lin countered, "The good news is that we pushed them hard twice now. They'll be jumping at every floor creak, worried that we've come to punch them in the face again."

Scarlett grinned at the martial words and the pictures they evoked. "How are our defenses?" It occurred to her that the Veil might not enjoy jumping at every floor squeak and might feel inspired to do something about it.

Wren replied, "Ready, willing, and able. We've even got the Riders on call. If the Veil is stupid enough to come here again, we'll clean their clocks for them."

Lin asked, "Did we get any leads, Amber?"

"I've been over the footage the drone took as it flew in,

frame by frame. Looks like only one bald baddie went down during the fight. Four others were there, and each had at least one assistant. I think one of them might have had an extra helper.

"The soldiers and guards were pretty generic. No facial recognition on them. None on the Veil either. Whoever they paid to wipe their traces from the web did a fine job of it."

Lin opened the box, extracted another piece of pizza, and dropped it on her plate. "So, what you're saying is no, no new leads."

Amber nodded. "No new leads. We still have Kingston Trane, though."

Wren cautioned, "We'll hold off on pursuing that for a couple of days. We need to let the fallout from this operation, well, fall out."

Everyone chuckled or smiled at the pun, and Scarlett replied, "Probably smart, but not all that rewarding."

The Witches' leader pushed her chair back and stood. "Unfortunately, my job isn't to make you all happy."

Lin replied in a fake whine, "But couldn't you try, just this once?"

Wren slapped her gently on the side of her head as she walked away. "No."

Lin faced the table and shrugged. "It was worth a try. What will you all do with your vacation time? I'll be tending bar and mending here, I guess."

Scarlett replied, "So, pretty much what you always do, then."

"Yeah. Pretty much. I live a generally happy life."

Runeclaw opened one eye and pinned Scarlett with it.

"If you say we're going to a tourist trap, I will murder you in your sleep."

Everyone laughed, and Scarlett replied, "No, not that. I think I'll spend some time with Diana and her team. Specifically, I'll ask Rath to teach me to throw knives. I missed badly during the fight." She frowned. "And now I've lost my wrist daggers again. Damn it to hell. Those were good."

Lin replied, "I'm sure Snow will enchant more for you."

Scarlett chuckled. "Remind me to tell you the lawn dart story."

Amber asked, "Rath? The troll?"

Scarlett nodded. "He's wicked sharp with daggers. Pun intended."

"Well. That's unexpected."

"Yeah, the agents are all full of surprises."

Lin asked, "How about you, Amber?"

The infomancer replied, "I'll be watching Trane's house. I'll also figure out how to break into it and what best to do once we're in there."

Lin immediately replied, "Kill him. That's best. Trust me on this."

"Maybe not. We'll see."

Wren shouted Lin's name across the bar, and the drow rolled her eyes. "Excuse me. The boss wants me to do something. Probably something stupid."

Scarlett asked, "What are you thinking about our friend Kingston Trane?"

Amber replied, "We need a lead. Maybe we can figure out a way to track him. Shoot him full of radioactive dye.

Implant something. I don't know, but the girl they captured gave me the idea."

Scarlett nodded. She liked the sound of that. "You have a plan?"

Amber shook her head. "No. I have a concept, at best. I'll be working hard to make it into an actual idea."

"If anyone can do it, it's you."

The other woman laughed. "I appreciate the vote of confidence."

Scarlett moved to the bar and chatted with the locals as Amber went to her normal booth to work. When she and Runeclaw returned to their room, she flopped down on the bed with a groan.

Runeclaw asked, "What's bothering you?"

"Aside from the fact that all our possible leads blew up?"

He flicked an ear as if to push the idea away. "Yes, aside from that."

She looked at the bedpost, where her dagger hung in its harness. "Fang."

Runeclaw tilted his head. "What's the matter?"

"I don't know if you saw it when I threw Fang at the dude in the gold robes. I was aiming for his shoulder. Everything in me was aiming for that shoulder. Yet when I threw it, it hit him perfectly in the throat, a flawless killing strike. I didn't want to kill him. I wanted to capture him."

"You think that's more than chance at work?"

Scarlett nodded. "I think Fang made it happen."

Runeclaw moved from a seated position to lying on all four paws. "You think the dagger is messing with you? Creeping into your brain? Taking control?"

Scarlett considered it, as she had many times before.

"Not really. What I think it is doing is influencing me at the moment of choice when it comes to killing people. Just pushing me across the line from wounding into killing. I'm not comfortable with that, especially when I don't realize it's happening in the moment."

"Understandable."

"So, while Rath teaches me to be better, I'll try throwing with Fang, too. We'll see how that goes. It might give me a little information one way or the other, anyway. And it's true that I need the practice."

Runeclaw laid his chin on his front paws. "You should shield your mind from it while you work."

"Good idea. Not sure I can, though."

"You can do anything you choose to."

Scarlett smiled at him. "How kind. Guardian wisdom? Random motivation?"

"No. I just know you."

"Are you being nice to me for some particular reason?" Her only answer was a snore, so she closed her eyes and followed the cat's wise example.

CHAPTER TWENTY

The next morning, Scarlett portaled them from the hotel to the landing room in the agents' base. She and Runeclaw spent several uncomfortable moments in the modest-sized chamber, then the door clicked several times and opened.

Cara smiled, and her dark eyes held more than a trace of amusement. "It's a little eerie in there, isn't it."

"Yes. Why is that?" Scarlett wondered if it was spelled.

"I think it's because it looks like an interrogation room or maybe a jail cell. Just triggers something subconscious when the doors are closed and locked."

Rath the troll, his purple hair sticking up in all directions and currently at his three-foot size, ran up behind Scarlett. He sprayed Runeclaw with a devastatingly accurate shot of water from a small plastic water pistol and ran off cackling. Runeclaw dashed after him.

Cara rolled her eyes. "I would've said it was impossible for Rath to be more trouble than he already was, but your cat seems to bring out the best in him. Or the worst."

"They're quite the pair, can't argue with that."

Cara took her through the facility and into Diana's office. The leader of the agents was behind the desk, working on a tablet, her medium-length brunette hair pulled back in a ponytail. She smiled and gestured at the chair across from her. "How's it going?"

Scarlett took the indicated chair as Cara perched on the edge of the desk. "We had a little tussle with the Luminous Veil. They had a facility where they were making those collars they use on captives. We dropped in on them in force. Big fight, killed one of the Veil principals, but the others got away. Then the place blew up."

Cara asked, "Do you mean you blew the place up?"

Scarlett shook her head. "No. It just blew up. We barely got out in time. Pretty sure some of the other side didn't."

Diana looked thoughtful. "Did someone use a spell? Like a fireball or something?"

"No. It was very similar to those videos I've seen of skyscrapers being imploded. Lots of little detonations, then a crash."

"They must've had the explosives in place before you got there, with the whole place carefully wired to go up. Why do you think they did that?"

Scarlett frowned. "Good question. I didn't think of that. And no one else mentioned it."

Cara observed, "Well, you were in the thick of things. It's understandable the big picture might have been a little murky from there."

"I guess they wanted to make sure no one knew they were there when they were done?"

Diana gave a sharp nod. "At least that. But what if it was more?"

"What more?"

"Like it was set up to kill off the people who were there once they were done with the collars."

Scarlett blinked at the surprising notion. "Factions within the Veil?"

Diana shrugged. "Maybe."

"Worth considering, anyway. Thanks for the thought."

"Don't mention it. What can we do for you today?"

Scarlett grinned. "Training."

Diana responded with a matching smile. "Our favorite thing."

"In knife throwing."

Cara groaned, and Scarlett shook her head. "Oh, you poor, poor person." She lifted her phone from the desk's surface, tapped a few buttons, and announced, "Whoever sees Rath, tell him to report to the knife range. Also tell him, must train."

Diana rose and motioned for Scarlett to follow as she headed through the doorway. They chatted as they walked through the facility to a room Scarlett remembered seeing but hadn't known its purpose.

Diana explained, "This is our knife range." Static targets in the shape of humanoid figures were mounted along the near wall, similar to those used on a shooting range. The rest of the space was devoted to an obstacle course, with the preferred route laid down in yellow paint on the white concrete.

Rath and Runeclaw ran in, and the troll grinned. "Knife

training. Most fun ever." He ran to a cabinet, pulled out a vest, and slipped it on. Six thin hilts of throwing knives stuck out of it, angled for easy reach.

As he pulled out a leather bandolier with more throwing knives on it, Scarlett asked, "What happens to the vest when he gets bigger?"

Diana replied, "Custom-made. It's breakaway. We can retrieve it after a fight as long as the place doesn't blow up around us."

The comment made Scarlett think of her lost throwing knives. She suppressed a growl of annoyance.

Rath handed her the bandolier, and she put it on, then pulled the strap to snug it tightly to her body. It contained six throwing knives, each blade pointing in an alternate direction to be drawn with the opposite hand. He said, "First, let's try static targets."

Scarlett adjusted the bandolier so it didn't interfere with Fang, then followed Rath's instructions. Her six throws with throwing knives all hit the target, and her throw with Fang struck true in the center.

Rath scolded, "You're just hitting anywhere. More focus. Be the knife." Scarlett asked what that meant. The troll grinned, then ran off to collect the knives from the target.

He handed them back, and she drew a deep breath to ready herself to throw again. "Be the knife, sure." Whether because she was warmed up or because the troll had cast some mysterious psychological spell with his words, all her throws were more accurate the second time.

Rath clapped. "Good. You're warmed up. Now we have

fun." They moved deeper into the room, and as they stood together on the starting line, Rath explained, "Don't hit the hostages. Go for wounding shots, not killing shots."

"Why?"

"Killing is easy. Wounding is hard. Practice to be better."

"Okay."

"We alternate. Don't stop running. I'll take the first."

Scarlett readied herself and took off as the troll glided into motion. The first target popped out almost immediately, a man holding a gun pointed at them. A knife left Rath's hands, spun in the air, and thudded into the target right where the man's hand gripped the pistol. Scarlett leapt over a low obstacle, dropped and rolled under a tall one, and came up to find another target in front of her. It depicted a family with two parents and four kids and a man holding a gun to one of the adults' heads.

Scarlett grabbed a blade with her right hand and hurled it. It struck the attacker in the shoulder, which she figured was good enough. The next few were the same, and Rath called instructions before her throws that she did her best to adapt to.

He finally yelled, "Last one," and Scarlett drew Fang instead of her sixth throwing knife. When the target popped open, it was a man with a rifle pointed at her. She threw, aiming for the man's leg. Fang thudded straight into the target's heart. She ran across the finish line, and Rath shook his head. "Kill shot. Be the knife."

Scarlett nodded. "Be the knife."

He grinned. "Now, cleanup." They collected the knives, and he asked, "Again?"

Scarlett shook her head. "Maybe later. I need to chat with Diana."

He nodded but reminded her, "Must train." Then he put the knives back in the locker, looked at Runeclaw, darted forward, and poked him in the side. "You're it." He ran off laughing with the cat in pursuit.

In the office, Diana asked how she thought it had gone.

"Pretty well. But I think my sentient dagger Fang is misbehaving."

Diana frowned. "How so?" Scarlett explained, and Diana nodded. "It can be a struggle. Sometimes the weapon seeks dominance. Sometimes it's willing to be a partner. You'll have to show it who's boss."

"Which means going into its space and having a conversation."

Diana chuckled. "If yours is anything like mine, it'll be a fight, not a conversation."

Scarlett nodded. "Yeah. Have any tips?"

"Do it in a safe place, with friends watching over you. People who know you well enough that if something weird happens and the dagger takes control of you, they'll recognize the change and assist."

"That can happen?"

Diana nodded as a grim expression turned her lips into a straight line. "That can happen. For the fight itself, you'll only have yourself to rely upon."

Scarlett fell back in her chair and let her arms hang as she stared at the ceiling. "I was afraid you'd say that."

The other woman laughed at the dramatic display. "Sorry. But there's no doubt in my mind you have what it takes to convince the dagger to behave."

"And if I can't?"

"We have plenty of cells here that are impervious to magic, where we can keep you until you beat it."

Scarlett looked at her, saw that she was entirely serious, and groaned. "Fantastic."

CHAPTER TWENTY-ONE

Scarlett headed straight to Wheels after leaving the agents' facility. Lin was seated across from Amber, each of them enjoying a soft drink. Scarlett asked, "Any updates?"

The infomancer replied, "Don't bother me. Working."

Lin rolled her eyes. "That's no, in Amber speak."

Scarlett chuckled. "I kind of figured. Are you free for a while?"

Lin rose. "Sure. What do you need?"

"Backup."

Her friend's demeanor went from playful to professional in a heartbeat. "Armed?"

Scarlett shook her head. "No. Just someone to watch over me while I do a thing."

"You got it."

They portaled to the Spell Riders' garage, said hello to Maddox, and headed to the back to find Snow. He was in his workshop as usual and grinned at the sight of them. "Well, look what the cat dragged in."

Runeclaw jumped onto his workbench and hissed softly. "You people need to stop with that joke, or there's gonna be a clawing."

Snow laughed. "Wondered how long it would take to annoy you." He fist-bumped each woman. "What can I do for you?"

Runeclaw replied, "Scarlett lost her throwing knives."

Scarlett winced. "That's not why we're here, but it is true."

Snow shook his head with a dramatic frown to show his feigned disappointment. "Careless."

"A building blew up on them."

"And you let it happen. So sad. Another set will cost you."

"How much?"

He grinned. "You come to the next cookout and bring a friend or two."

She laughed. "Done."

"So, what is it you need?"

"To use your protective circle. My dagger's being problematic, and I need to have a chat with it."

A slight frown appeared on Snow's face. "That can be kind of dangerous. Do you think you'll be safe?"

"As I understand it, I should be. Unless, of course, the being inside the dagger completely devours my personality and takes over. That's why she's here." She jerked her head toward Lin.

The drow crossed her arms. "You might've explained that beforehand. I could have had an opinion."

"Which is why I didn't explain it beforehand."

Snow stood. "Of course you can use it. Is there anything else I can do?"

"If you have time, I guess you can back up Lin. But I have no idea how long this will take."

"Consider it done." He escorted them to the small room devoted to his need for occasional magical protection. He explained to her how to invoke the magic of the circle and took out the box containing the collar they'd found.

Scarlett asked, "Does the collar need to be in the circle when it's in the box?"

Snow replied, "Belt and suspenders. Redundancy is good when it comes to defense."

Lin remarked, "I like the way you think."

He grinned. "Thinking is what I do best."

Scarlett sat in the circle and looked at the others. "Wish me luck." Before she could close it, Runeclaw hopped in. She ruffled his fur and warned, "You might not want to be here for this."

He countered, "And you might need me. I'm staying." He crawled over her crossed legs into her lap and curled up there. "Whenever you're ready. Time's wasting."

"You're something, cat." She closed the circle's wards with the wand in her left hand. Then she drew Fang from its sheath along her ribs. The dagger's presence immediately touched her mind. She laid the dagger on her knee, put her left hand on her other knee, and arranged the objects she held so they were touching. "Here we go."

She sensed the route that would take her down into the dagger to commune with the entity inside it. Before traveling it, she focused her magic and created connections. First, her power leapt through the pendant, the touchstone to her grandmother, and a potential source of unknown power. She was pretty sure its magic had already been exhausted, but it eased her mind to connect to it.

From there, she sent her magic into the connection through the pendant on Runeclaw's harness to deepen her link with the cat. His presence would help ground her. Only then did she send her power into the dagger.

It felt for several seconds like being in free fall with the ground rushing up at her. Then suddenly she was standing on parched earth with the cracks in the dirt under her feet radiating out in all directions.

A sound from behind caused her to turn, and she saw Fang. She never saw the dagger's avatar appear. It was always just there when she turned.

The snake had coiled its tail and used it as a platform to reach a height greater than hers. It looked like a cobra with wariness and malevolence in its eyes, tempered with a touch of humor. The fact that it was unchanged since the last time she met it was reassuring. The fangs it displayed were less so. The snake hissed, "Wielder."

Scarlett nodded. "Fang."

"What has brought you here? It is lovely to see you, of course, and you are always welcome." His tone suggested a touch of resentment, and she wasn't sure if it was because she hadn't been to visit or because she was there now.

"I sense that you've been influencing me."

The snake bowed a little, his muscles rippling in his body. "Of course. We are partners. You will always draw upon my advice."

Scarlett shook her head. "Not what I meant. I threw to wound during the last battle in order to capture an enemy.

I don't think I messed up the throw, but you didn't go where I wanted you to."

Fang's look of confusion was too intense to be real. "Why would you throw to wound? Why risk that?"

His defensive attitude brought out her defensiveness. "I had my reasons."

Fang hissed, "That you refuse to articulate."

Scarlett waved it off. "The details aren't relevant. If you're suborning my will, that's a problem."

He smiled, which somehow made the fangs look bigger. "Suborning is such a big word."

"Will you stop?"

The smile widened. "Prove you are worthy." His attack came without warning. One moment he was standing. The next he was in motion toward her, his entire body expanding as he launched himself through the air.

Scarlett snapped shields around herself with an effort of will since she needed no representation of her wand to perform magic in this place. She blasted force magic into the ground to launch herself away from the snake's attack. He redirected instantly and slithered toward her as she landed. She thrust out her hand and dispatched a bolt of force that slammed into the snake and slowed but failed to stop him.

Scarlett extended her magic into her hands. Knives materialized in her grips, made entirely of force magic with wickedly sharp edges and points that only magic could create. As Fang reached her, she spun and danced aside from its effort to bite her neck. She slashed both knives down as she twirled away, then leapt over the tail that tried to bludgeon her and sliced him on the other side.

Scarlett sprinted to a safe distance, turned back to see how much damage she'd dished out, and discovered all she'd managed to do was scratch his scales. His laughter was haughty and mocking. "Such puny weapons. If only you had teeth like mine."

Scarlett clapped her hands together, then turned them palm-out to face him. A cone of focused flame bounded by force magic reached out. He dodged at first, but she maintained the blast and traversed it across to catch him. The scales it struck grew dark, clearly damaged, and he hissed in anger. "Foolish witch."

"Stupid snake."

He charged, and this time Scarlett ran to meet him. She pumped magic into her muscles, and as his head darted forward to attack, she leapt upward in a jumping kick. Her spin delivered a wicked roundhouse blow to his head and carried her past him. She landed cleanly, ready to fight, as he turned, looking dazed.

Scarlett grinned with real pleasure at this moment of success, then paid for her distraction as his tail whipped around to smack her in the side of the head. She staggered backward and fell, barely managing to keep the back of her skull from smashing into the ground. Darkness closed in at the edges of her vision and took it all away.

CHAPTER TWENTY-TWO

Scarlett's vision returned to normal, and she realized she'd been unconscious for only a second or two. The snake was in motion, and only as Scarlett threw herself out of the way did she realize a hiss in her ear had woken her up. She guessed the snake had hissed, although doing so would've been a stupid choice under the circumstances. Well, maybe it had been a mistake, in which case she'd take it. Or perhaps it was Fang playing with her, in which case she'd enjoy showing him how foolish a choice that was.

She reached her feet, then cartwheeled to the side barely in time to avoid another strike from Fang's tail aimed at her temple. In this space, her motions were crafted from will rather than physical exertion. She could do acrobatics she would have been hard-pressed to pull off in the real world and never would have tried during a fight. Nonetheless, she threaded magic into her muscles as she would have in a regular fight to increase her speed and reflexes.

Scarlett bared her teeth at the snake. "Hit a girl while

she's down? Rude. Let's see how you like this." She raised her left hand and blasted a beam of fire at the snake, aimed slightly off-center to that side. An instant later, she sent a cone of electricity out from her right hand, a tightly bound spiral of sparks that expanded into forks of lightning as it traveled.

Fang dodged the fire as she'd expected him to do, with a move in the opposite direction that put him squarely in the path of her electricity.

The sparks covered him. They sizzled and snapped as they attacked his scales. He fell to the ground and slithered out of the way faster than she could track him with the beam, so she let it lapse. When he straightened again, several more scales were burned and blackened. She laughed. "So, not indestructible. Good to know."

Now that she'd confirmed electricity could damage him, she had a plan. She coated her arms and legs with extra force magic, then added lightning to her fists and feet. Scarlett charged the snake, and he reared up, ready to bite. She jumped and landed a roundhouse kick to the side of his face as he extended to bite her.

The blow knocked him sideways, and she landed cleanly and spun into another kick. Her heel passed over his head as he dropped to the ground. She jumped back into a handspring, flipping several times to get out of his way, then landed cleanly in a fighting stance with a laugh of pure pleasure. "Oh, I like fighting here."

Fang let out a long hiss that sounded different than the one that had awoken her, then a stream of venom flew out of his mouth at her.

She circled her hands inward, and two cones of frost

met the venom, which froze before it could reach her. Scarlett moved her hands in midair, crafting and shaping, and the frozen venom turned into an icicle that spun and shot at the snake. She charged in after it as it flew.

Her projectile slammed into his tail, then into the parched earth, pinning him momentarily. It gave her time to deliver three punches to his face and a kick to his body that rocked him backward. She backpedaled as he flicked his tail and the iced venom broke. The drops landed on the ground and sank in. She asked, "Ready to give up?"

An arrogant smile accompanied a snarl. Then Fang broke apart into a dozen smaller snakes. Scarlett backpedaled as she used her magic to throw lightning, frost, and fire at the smaller targets. The little buggers were quick and evaded three out of four shots as they closed on her. She felt a tug at the corner of her mind, realized what it was, and laughed as she opened her thoughts to it.

Runeclaw appeared on the ground beside her, and she coated the cat in force protection as he ran toward the nearest snake. His teeth closed on its neck, and he violently shook his head until his prey vanished as vapor.

Scarlett continued her attacks, keeping the ones attacking her at bay and firing spells at any that ignored her to distract them while Runeclaw eliminated them one by one.

When the last one had evaporated, Fang reappeared. He frowned at the cat, then at her. "Very strange. No one has ever been able to do that before."

Scarlett shrugged. "Perhaps no one has ever had such a vexing partner before."

Runeclaw replied, "Nasty."

She countered, "True."

Runeclaw blasted lightning from his tail. It caught Fang by surprise since their bickering had distracted him. The snake roared, and Scarlett added blasts of electricity and fire to the mix. He dodged her attack and managed to avoid Runeclaw's but was decidedly on the defensive.

Runeclaw continued to try to hit Fang from afar while Scarlett dashed in to fist and foot range. She shoved her force-protected arm up into Fang's mouth as he tried to bite her and used the other one to pummel his body, which caused him to break off and retreat.

He continued to retreat from their attacks. Although the space was too large and wide open for them to corner it, the situation was definitely in their favor. One mistake, and they would have him. Scarlett yelled, "Do you yield?"

The snake stopped, and his familiar arrogant smile appeared. "I do. You are worthy. I will not influence you unless you ask for my help."

Scarlett felt the energy of combat wash out of her. "Was that really so hard?"

He laughed. "Not for me."

Scarlett closed her eyes, and when she opened them, she was back in the real world. She slipped the dagger back into its sheath, deactivated the wards with her wand, and returned her wand to her sleeve. Lin asked, "You okay?"

Scarlett groaned and extended a hand to the drow. "Tired."

As Lin pulled her up, Runeclaw interjected, "I saved her. As usual."

Scarlett confirmed, "He helped. I've come to a new arrangement with Fang. It's all good."

Snow asked, "You're confident the dagger will keep its word?"

"I'm confident it will keep its word for a time, anyway. After that, I guess we'll have to see."

"Fair enough. I wish I could offer the use of some magic to offset it, but I'm afraid I've got nothing."

Scarlett laughed. "Yeah, neither do I."

"On the plus side, I have enchanted throwing daggers for you."

"Already?"

He grinned. "Well, you lose them so often that I already had backups. Figured they'd come in handy eventually." Runeclaw laughed, and Lin chuckled as they walked to Snow's area. He presented her with throwing daggers. "These are on the house. After this, you're going to have to start paying."

"Or start beating up people with throwing daggers and taking them, right?"

He grinned. "I didn't say these came from our room of defeated opponents' gear, did I?"

She slipped them into a pocket. "Thank you, as always."

"Don't mention it."

Scarlett's phone buzzed, and she glanced at Lin.

The other woman looked down at hers as it buzzed too. "We need to get back right away. Amber has something for us."

CHAPTER TWENTY-THREE

They portaled back to Wheels after saying goodbye to Maddox and Snow. The bartender pointed them toward Amber's normal spot. As Scarlett slid into the booth opposite her, Amber grumbled, "You're back, finally."

Scarlett replied, "What's the rush?"

Amber absentmindedly reached up to pat Runeclaw, who was rubbing his face against the side of her laptop screen. "Spotted Kingston Trane through a window at his house. It's the first time I've been able to verify his presence in the place. No idea how long he'll be there, though."

Lin summarized, "So you're saying we have to move now."

"That's exactly what I'm saying."

Excitement banished any remaining tiredness from Scarlett's fight against her dagger. "What's the plan?"

Amber leaned back, and Runeclaw jumped into her lap to receive additional petting. "I've come up with something to track him with. It's a liquid-based material. The problem is getting it onto him without him knowing."

Scarlett asked, "Can it be put in a dart?"

Lin bumped her shoulder hard. "He'd probably notice a dart sticking out of him, you know?"

Scarlett scowled. "Fair. But you're a jerk."

Amber added, "It has to be subtle. Anything that comes off as the least bit suspicious might result in Trane being cut out of the Veil since we've already got them worried. They're likely to overreact."

Lin replied, "So, something sneaky is required."

Scarlett nodded. "I can be sneaky."

Runeclaw jumped onto the table. "I can do this. You make something I can wear that will shoot the stuff, and Scarlett can get me inside. I'll take it from there."

Scarlett observed, "Could be dangerous."

Runeclaw gave her his patented condescending look. "You're about as sneaky as a rhinoceros."

"Like you've seen a rhinoceros."

"I know they're loud and stomp around a lot. Just like you do."

Lin laughed. "I think he's got you there."

"I don't like either of you."

Amber countered, "I don't have a better plan, do either of you?"

Lin and Scarlett both shook their heads. Runeclaw declared, "So. Let's do this thing."

As dusk fell, the preparations were finally in place. Lin and Amber had collaborated on creating a quasi-armor piece for Runeclaw. The matte black fabric covered part of his right side, and straps went across his torso and around his neck to hold it in place. A small nozzle and bottle that matched the fabric were mounted on it.

As Scarlett got it settled around him and secured the straps, she asked, "How does it work?"

Amber replied, "The nozzle is activated by that cord there." She pointed at it. "Runeclaw can pull it with a paw when he wants. We tested it out, and it works fine."

"What's inside it?"

"A radioactive isotope that emits on a rare wavelength. It won't be picked up on anything standard, but I can program several scientific satellites to search that band. We'll know where the liquid is if it all works as expected. I've already made a map of all the other places where the isotope naturally occurs so we can eliminate them from our oversight. The substance decays pretty quickly and will be gone after a week."

Lin had left bartending to join them as they got the cat ready. "If it takes longer than that to get something useful, we go the less sneaky route, grab him, and beat the information out of him."

Amber replied, "Which risks the Veil changing their plans. Let's just hope it works, shall we?"

Runeclaw declared, "It'll work. Let's get it done. Listening to you all talk is boring."

A Witch waiting for them outside portaled them as near to the house as the Witches had been willing to venture during their surveillance.

This last piece of cover was a copse of trees partway up the long driveway. The house was a grand structure, two stories high but much wider than most Scarlett had seen. It had columns and pretty windows. The yellow that complemented the white was so vibrant it looked like the building had been painted that day.

Scarlett adjusted the straps of the anti-magic backpack she'd brought on the off chance it might be useful and those of the bulky sensor pack tethered to her belt and a loop around her thigh.

Her display glasses filled with information as Amber used the sensor packs she and Runeclaw carried to scan the area. Amber reported, "Wired alarms on all the windows. I can keep the call from going out, but I can't do anything with whatever internal warnings might be connected to them."

Scarlett frowned. "No network?"

"No."

"Weird."

"Some houses have it set up so network access is only available at the moment of use. That's the smart approach for security purposes. It means they have dedicated devices for entertainment, which have a continuous connection, but I can't use that to get anywhere useful."

Scarlett growled, "Jerks."

Amber laughed. "Yeah, that's my opinion, too. Too smart for our good."

Runeclaw observed, "They've proven to be competent enemies all along. Not a surprise that they continue to be."

Amber explained, "The yellow is magic detection. It's all over the house. Blue is motion. Red is acoustic. You can see the cameras' arcs."

Scarlett nodded. The areas the camera could see were drawn in crosshatched white on the image. She focused on the connection she'd automatically maintained with

Runeclaw and retracted it so it wouldn't set off those magic sensors. In all probability, it wouldn't be a powerful enough magic to be detected, but it didn't seem smart to take any unnecessary risk.

Runeclaw asked, "Are you ready yet?"

Scarlett frowned at him. "Don't be a jerk. Are you?"

"Absolutely."

"All right then. Go for it. I'll guide you when I can."

They had discussed giving him appropriately sized goggles with the same display she had in her glasses so he could see the zones himself, but he hadn't wanted them. Scarlett and Runeclaw had done this before and were both comfortable with what it took for her to talk him through the sensor fields.

Her display glasses' magnification allowed her to track him as he crossed the lawn, keeping low and moving naturally through the shadows where there were shadows available. The closest thing on their side was a garage attached to the main structure, and at her whispered question, Amber confirmed the windows and doors of the garage were also wired.

Scarlett asked, "Do you see anything yet?"

Runeclaw replied, "No. Nothing that will get us into the garage."

"So how are you planning to get in?"

"Very carefully."

While they'd hoped they might come upon an open window that would give Runeclaw access to the place, they hadn't relied on it. Amber had watched the house for long enough to know that a guard would come outside several times during the night to patrol the grounds. The schedule was irregular, but it had happened multiple times every evening while they'd had the house under surveillance, and it hadn't happened yet that evening. As long as the guards maintained their routine, Runeclaw had a possible way into the house.

Scarlett watched as he took up a position near the door the guards had used most often. If it was the one they used tonight, he would sneak in as the guard came out. If it wasn't, he'd have to follow the guard around and sneak through as he reentered the house. They'd all prefer the former, but he was prepared for the latter.

Their luck was good that night. Ten minutes later, the door creaked open. The guard paused to say something to another person inside, then laughed. As he turned away and pulled the door closed behind him, Runeclaw shot through and out of sight.

Scarlett whispered, "He's inside. Let's hope Trane doesn't have a dog, or this could get messy."

CHAPTER TWENTY-FOUR

After dashing inside, Runeclaw ducked into the shadows, what little there were of them, by running under a small table near the door. He had to crouch to squeeze under it, but he was a flexible cat and managed it without incident. His keen eyes watched as feet moved around the room, presumably owned by whoever the guard had been talking to, then walked away out of sight.

His whiskers wiggled as he sniffed and found no trace of anyone or anything else nearby. A tiny voice emerged from the speaker beside the camera mounted on his chest harness near his pendant.

Amber advised, "This looks like it was once a mudroom or something but has been beefed up for security's use. I see motion sensors, cameras, and audio sensors present in the room, but all at low power. No anti-magic emitter nor magic detection is present."

Scarlett added, "I'm not going to risk trying to magically connect with you unless you really want it. I doubt the sensors outside would detect it, but since we haven't tested it, we don't know. If you want me to activate it, wave your paw in front of the camera, or if it's safe to do so, tell me through the microphone." He moved slightly up and down, so the camera nodded for him.

Amber reported, "Picking up some thermals in the next rooms. Can't tell if they're guards, workers, or what, but they're vertical and moving. We've also got one moving upstairs, plus several horizontal figures."

Scarlett quipped, "Dare we hope it's a Veil sleepover, and we can get them all?"

Runeclaw refrained from telling her how stupid that comment was and settled for a soft hiss that caused the channel to go quiet. He crept out from under the table and took stock of his surroundings.

The white-painted room had a row of cabinets mounted up high that traveled from the exterior wall, along a side wall, and to the opening that led out of the room opposite the door. Pegs were mounted in the walls, a couple supporting light jackets, and two benches were set at right angles in the corner.

The room was very clean, lending to Amber's idea that a cleaning crew might be at work. He spotted a glint of metal above the cabinets and moved cautiously to the side before making a small jump up to the table. He froze until Amber reported, "You didn't set off the detectors. Maybe they're not active in the room since guards move through it. Still, be careful. For all we know, they could turn back on at any time."

Runeclaw made another jump to the top of the cabinets. He walked along them to the corner, then to the next corner, and stopped at a metal grate set into the interior wall. He slipped a claw behind it and carved through the plaster around one of the screws holding the panel in place. He peered inside and discovered the metal ductwork went back only a short distance before turning down. His goal was upstairs, so that wouldn't be a viable route.

Runeclaw retraced his steps back to the floor, then moved beside the doorway leading out. He stuck his head around the wall and found a hallway going to the right and another room across from the one he was in.

Amber advised, "You've got stairs up three rooms ahead. There's someone in the next room, so be careful."

Runeclaw peeked in all directions to ensure no one would see him, then crossed into the next room and slipped under the nearest piece of furniture, a chest of drawers. The chamber was a dining room. A long table covered with an expensive-looking cloth dominated the center of the space. Tall glass display cabinets held more kinds of dishes than he'd known existed, and he imagined the matching low storage unit he crouched under held other items relevant to hosting fancy dinner parties.

A woman in a black uniform walked briskly through the room with a feather duster that she ran over all the exposed surfaces. Runeclaw waited, watched, and hoped she would move on to dust another room rather than changing tasks in this one. He readied himself to blast her if she saw him as she headed for the doorway he'd come through, but she walked out of the room and turned down the hallway without noticing anything amiss.

He waited several seconds to be sure she wouldn't turn around right away, then crawled slowly along the wall, moving under each piece of furniture as he navigated the room's perimeter.

When he reached the opening in the far wall, Amber confirmed, "Thermals say that room's clear."

He moved into it slowly to avoid setting off the motion detector, which might be active since no one was in the room. He didn't know how Amber was dealing with the house's cameras but figured she'd done something to compromise them. If not, maybe whoever was supposed to be watching them wasn't paying attention or thought a cat wandering through the house was normal. He didn't smell any other cats, but who knew?

The mission's lack of certainty was a challenge but one he was uniquely prepared for. He was a guardian, and what was more, he excelled at thinking on his feet. Whatever came up, he'd deal with it.

Amber prompted, "Okay, shoot across the hallway. The stairs are on your left on the other side of that wall."

Runeclaw peered around the corner and froze. A guard appeared and turned to go up the stairs without looking down. Runeclaw let out a slow breath. If the guard had continued forward, he would have been unlikely to remain unseen. While he'd use his lightning if he needed to, as Amber had warned, it might cause this lead to be snipped off.

Scarlett suggested, "Maybe wait for the guard to get all the way upstairs before you follow."

Runeclaw made a few cutting comments in his mind but refrained from vocalizing them. He crept up the stairs one by one, careful to stay at the edge where he would be least likely to be spotted by someone on the floor above. As he reached the second-floor corridor, he heard the guard moving off to the left. A knob turned with a *squeak*, and a door opened with the sound of wood brushing across thick carpet.

Runeclaw crossed the corridor and dashed through the cracked door on the opposite side. The room turned out to be a study, with a massive wooden desk, several stuffed chairs that looked eminently clawable, and several other attractive ornaments and expensive pieces of furniture.

He crept under a chair with fabric that went down to the floor on all sides. The cat peered out through the tiny crack in the corner as the guard walked in, traveled a circuit of the room, made some silly noises, and exited.

Runeclaw stepped out from under the chair and looked up. Suspended from the ceiling was an ornate gold cage with two birds inside, one yellow and green, one blue and white. They weren't large birds, but the cage still seemed small and inadequate for them. He jumped onto the chair to get a better look.

Amber chided, "Ignore the birds. You're on a mission."

Runeclaw thought, *Birds aren't pets. They need to fly. Imprisoning them in such a tiny space is cruel.*

He jumped onto the bookshelf, then readied his muscles for a larger leap.

Amber warned again, "Don't," but he ignored her. There wouldn't be active motion sensors this soon after the guard's exit, so it was now or never.

He launched across the intervening space and grabbed the cage door with his claws. The impact was enough to tear it open, and he dropped from the swaying golden prison. The birds looked down and chirped at him but didn't leave despite their ability to do so. He shook his head, muttered, "Stupid birds," and headed for the door.

Amber guided him toward the bedroom she thought was Trane's. The door was closed when he reached it, but fortunately had a lever rather than a knob. He probably could have cut through the latch if he had to, but it would've been difficult and potentially noisy. He leapt, grabbed the lever long enough for it to click open, then dropped to the floor and froze. No reaction came.

He pushed the door open, ensured it was almost closed in case the guard spotted it, and crossed the room to where light snoring came from a bed. He jumped gently onto the mattress and found not one figure but two. The bald man he had come for was lying beside a woman about his age with his arm wrapped around her. Her hair was still present, and Runeclaw wondered if that made Trane jealous. He leaned over to look at the woman's neck but saw no sign that she was collared.

Scarlett must've been thinking along the same lines because she whispered, "Guess there really is someone for everyone."

Amber cautioned, "Wait one," and Runeclaw crouched, not knowing what was going on. A moment later, she added, "Can't hack his phone. We hate competent enemies. Do what you came to do, buddy."

Runeclaw moved up the bed to the back of the man's head and positioned the nozzle. He extended his paw toward the small ring, hooked a claw around it, then pulled. The trackable spray hissed out onto the man's head and neck.

Amber had assured him the delivery was so subtle that

it was unlikely to be noticed even if he'd applied it while Trane was awake. Still, Runeclaw leapt to the floor, crawled under the bed, and waited to see if any reaction occurred.

When nothing changed in the breathing of those on the bed after half a minute, he headed back toward the door. On the way, he noticed an opening leading to a walk-in closet and detoured to spray the tracer over all of the man's shoes.

Scarlett commented, "Good thinking, now get out."

Runeclaw moved carefully back through the house and did his best to keep to the shadows. Now that his work was done, he wished he could make the nozzle apparatus disappear so he'd look like a normal cat if someone spotted him. When he reached the room he'd first entered, he crouched under the same piece of furniture and waited for someone to open the door.

A small chirp from above caught his attention. The birds had also made it to this room and were looking down from the top of the cabinets. They weren't looking at him specifically but pivoted their heads around in all directions like they sought an escape from the room and the house.

The *click* of the door a moment later propelled Runeclaw into motion. He dashed between the guard's legs as he stepped in but twisted at the last minute and threw his body against the man's foot as it rose to take a step.

The guard fell, and the door banged open with a loud crash. The startled birds flew out with a screech. Runeclaw silently laughed as he dashed into the grass, crouched, and froze, a black cat in a black night. The guard looked out the door once he reached his feet with an expression of annoyance twisting his face, then shook his head and went inside.

Runeclaw moved carefully back to the tree line as Amber and Scarlett steered him around the many sensors guarding the grounds around the house. When he reached her, Scarlett asked, "What was the deal with the birds?"

Runeclaw gave her a haughty look in response to the comment. "Birds are prey, not pets."

Scarlett raised an eyebrow. "Oh. That's why. Prey. Sure."

He countered, "Shouldn't you be shutting up, and shouldn't we be getting out of here?"

Scarlett laughed. "Can't argue with that. Good work, buddy. Let's go."

CHAPTER TWENTY-FIVE

Camus stood in his bedroom and stared at himself in the mirror. He wore the dark suit and crimson tie he donned for normal, everyday engagements but would soon be in what he considered his true self's attire. Lines of stress were visible around his eyes and at the corners of his mouth that kept wanting to turn down.

Tonight's ceremony was a pivotal moment in his plan. The subjects were ready. The collars were ready. It was time to merge the two, after which only a few steps would remain until he fulfilled his plan.

He checked them off mentally. The gathering. Eliminating his opposition within Veil. Then exerting his control over those who had brought a collared servant to their home.

He forced a smile and turned to face Katie, who stood nearby with her hands extended. He shrugged out of his jacket, handed it to her, and patted her on the head as she moved away to hang it up. It was good to have her back, and better that the witch and her friends hadn't been able to damage her after they'd taken her.

He undid his tie and hung it on the cabinet door for her to deal with when she finished arranging his jacket, then opened the door and headed down the hallway. Ellis moved from where he stood beside the door and fell into step with him. The bodyguard wore body armor and visible weapons.

Camus asked, "Is the site prepared?"

"It is."

Their path took them down the stairs. "Any chance it's been discovered?"

"None." Ellis' voice held complete confidence. "We researched and prepared several potential locations, which was labor-intensive but ensured no one would know which would be chosen. I selected this one myself only an hour ago. I immediately messaged everyone the details, but they'll be scrambling to make it there on time, and no one will be able to get word out with the location in time for a response. Even then, I didn't give them the actual place, just somewhere to report to. My people will portal them the rest of the way."

Camus smiled at his subordinate's thoroughness. "Very good." When they reached the cellar, he went through the complicated steps to open the door to his sanctuary. Once inside, he moved to the large wardrobe on one wall. Ellis took a position by the door, his hands naturally finding their appropriate spots on the rifle on his chest.

Camus removed the armor pieces from the armor stand one by one and donned them, leaving the helmet behind as always. Next, he retrieved his ceremonial robes and slid them on over the armor. He checked in the mirror to ensure the armor that was the Veil leaders' legacy was fully concealed, then cast a spell to help hide the slight noise it made. It sounded like a rustle of fabric but a little different than ordinary.

Finally, he took out his battle staff, cast the illusion that would make it appear to be his normal staff, and set it against the side of the cabinet. He moved to another piece of furniture similar to an apothecary's cabinet with larger drawers, cast a spell to unlock it, and pulled two drawers open. From each, he extracted a glass vial and held them up to the light to inspect them before sliding them into hardened loops on his armor's belt that would protect them.

Ellis asked, "What are those?"

Camus turned to face him. "Wizard's grenades."

The other man frowned. "I've never heard of such a thing."

Camus offered a thin smile. "Each contains some nasty things that can be activated with the right touch of magic. They took significant time to create, which is why I don't carry them except in the most important circumstances. Given our recent experiences, it seems prudent to have them with us."

Ellis nodded. "Makes sense."

Camus retrieved his staff and slid his wand into the forearm sheath where it could be in his hand in an instant. "What is the situation at the site?"

"I detailed only my most trusted people to guard, but reserves are a portal away. No one except me and the persons doing the portaling know exactly where we'll be."

Camus nodded. "Again, excellent." He gripped the staff

in both hands and cast the spells that would ready him for the ceremony. First, he layered a skintight force shield around himself, then added another at a slightly greater distance. He enhanced his senses and pumped the slightest bit of additional energy into his muscles. He didn't want to overuse his magic on unnecessary preparation, but he couldn't afford to be vulnerable.

Finally, he grabbed healing and energy potions from a rack that contained several of each and tucked one of each into the opposite side of his belt from the vials. "I'm ready. Are the subjects and collars in place?"

Ellis touched his ear and echoed that question. A moment later, he nodded. "They are."

"Good. Let's get this done."

Scarlett and Lin sat together at Wheels' bar, sipping bottles of beer and chatting about inconsequential things. It had been several days since the break-in to Kingston Trane's house, and nothing had yet come of it. The tension grew with each day that passed since they all knew eventually something had to break. The waiting was a grind, but it was better than having no hope.

When the break arrived, it came in the form of all the phones in the room suddenly buzzing, beeping, or giving some other signal. Scarlett grabbed hers and stared at it. The group message contained only the words **Prom dress**. Scarlett grinned.

Lin muttered, "All right. About time."

They portaled to the warehouse, and most of the

people in Wheels funneled through the portal to join them. Once the flow had stopped, they headed to their lockers and geared up for whatever Wren had planned for them.

Scarlett donned her usual stuff—the base black uniform, the belt that held a few grenades, a holster for her revolver, Fang's harness, her sensor pack, and the brick that acted as a communication relay. She slotted its companion earpiece into her ear and heard several conversations going on. Excitement filled the channel as everyone prepared.

After she put on the body armor Lin always insisted she wear, the harness for her long knives went over her head next. Once it was in place, she checked the draw over her shoulders. They were ready. She added the wrist sheaths with the throwing knives she hadn't had a chance to practice with yet. Given that Snow had created them, she was sure they would be excellent.

The bandolier with its six tranquilizer darts went on over it all, then she slipped on her leather jacket, touched her wand to ensure it was in the right place, grabbed the anti-magic backpack, and strapped it on.

Lin commented, "You complain about the body armor, but you'll carry that thing around."

Scarlett grinned. "We're better equipped to fight other magicals in the absence of magic than they are us."

Lin frowned. "I don't know if those words go together like that. But if you're saying we're tougher than them, I can't argue. Rifle?"

Scarlett shook her head. "Not this time."

"This once, I won't fight you on it." Lin crossed the

room to select a rifle and returned with it slung over her shoulders.

Wren walked into the room and clapped to get everyone's attention as she stepped up on a bench to address them all. "Our boy left the house for the first time in days. He's gone through several portals, doubtless to throw off pursuit.

"Amber is tracking him. As soon as he comes to rest for more than five minutes, we're on our way. Get your bikes ready. We'll probably have some distance to cover from whatever portal we have closest."

Ten minutes later, one of the Witches opened a portal. Scarlett passed through to see Cara from Diana Sheen's team on the other side.

The other woman grinned. "I have the closest portal." She waved to open a rift.

The Witches pushed their bikes through, then rode with Wren in the lead and Scarlett somewhere in the middle. A trio of drones had whipped through the portal a short time after the first motorcycle had passed through and fed images into Scarlett's display glasses.

Amber spoke. "All right. I've got the location nailed down. It's the building on top of the hill, only accessible by a winding road up one side. No cover at all."

Wren replied, "Damn. Okay. Let me know when we're near." When they were about a mile away, Wren ordered, "Veil."

Everyone cast the spells to hide their motorcycles and watched extra carefully for any other traffic. They got onto the winding road without a problem and rolled toward the top of the giant hill or maybe a small mountain.

The road was several miles long, always climbing, and switched back on itself several times. The image in Scarlett's display glasses showed a medium-sized two-story building with a huge metal antenna beside it. "What is that?"

Amber replied, "Records show it used to be a television station, but it shut down a long time ago when everything went to streaming."

Wren asked, "Defenses?"

A new window opened in their glasses to show the building in the center and colored areas around it. "All the usual detection kinds around the grounds. No sign of magic detection in the building itself."

"Makes it that much more likely it's our place. He's inside?"

"Satellite says he's either in there or within a hundred yards of it. Thermals show nobody outside, but they might be using cooling suits to hide themselves."

Scarlett could hear Wren's frown. "We can't go up under a veil or the magic will be detected, which loses us the element of surprise. Any active defenses?"

"None visible, but electrical signals are running all over the place outside the building."

"Damn it. They'll get away if we can't strike them by surprise."

Unexpectedly, Runeclaw interjected, "I have an idea to get us to the roof."

Scarlett relayed over the comm, "I might have an idea. Hang on." Runeclaw explained, and Scarlett shook her head at the cat perched on the motorcycle in front of her. "Never call me crazy again."

"Is that a yes?"

Scarlett explained the plan over the comm. "Anyone have a better idea?"

None did, and Wren instructed, "Okay. We'll go with that. Pull over here. I'll select some people to portal back for gear. Amber, watch for enemy drones. Everyone else, stay hidden until we're ready to move. The more we can shock these bastards with our arrival, the better."

CHAPTER TWENTY-SIX

Runeclaw waited as the Witches threw gear through portals from the warehouse to the area where they'd parked their motorcycles. The whole space was still protected under a veil to keep them from being noticed by prying eyes. A drone idled about two feet off the ground beside him.

Scarlett asked, "Are you sure you want to do this?"

"You know it's the only way."

"It's also quite dangerous."

"It'll be fine."

She shook her head as she knelt to look into his eyes. "I thought you'd be the conservative one. But no, you're the loose cannon. A wild card."

He snorted. "You need to quit watching silly old movies."

Scarlett reached out and ensured the harness holding his pendant was secure, then waved her wand. The connection between them strengthened. "If anything goes wrong, if an alarm goes off, if you're in danger, you find safety. It's not worth losing you to accomplish this."

"Will do."

Amber announced, "Ready on my end."

Wren handed Scarlett a coil of black rope, which she looped over her shoulder and neck, and asked, "You sure about this, cat?"

"Yep."

"Then we're ready. Take it away, you two."

Runeclaw jumped onto the drone, which wobbled under his weight as he quickly found his balance. Scarlett stared at him, stared at the drone, and said with some evident reluctance, "He's good to go."

Amber replied, "Moving."

Runeclaw crouched on the drone as it flew toward the building. He knew other drones were around somewhere looking for things that might threaten him, but he couldn't see what they were doing. He had to trust that Amber knew her stuff. She usually did.

His part of the plan was simple since it only required him to reach the roof. He and Scarlett had used her ability to teleport to his location on several other occasions. The only question here was whether he could find a spot away from cameras and whether magic used above the magic detection sensor on the roof of the building would register.

If it did, he would fight off whoever came toward him long enough for Scarlett to open the portal. He figured despite what she'd said, she knew he wasn't likely to run.

His thoughts were interrupted as Amber warned, "Hold on. There's someone up in the tower." His drone slowed and shifted into hover mode.

Wren asked, "Are your drones armed?"

"The one Runeclaw's riding is."

Runeclaw suggested, "Get me close enough, and I can blast him with lightning." Scarlett echoed the words.

Amber asked, "Can you do it without hitting the drone?"

Scarlett captured his annoyance as she echoed his response. "Of course."

"All right. Here we go."

The drone swooped in toward the tall antenna. He saw the man crouched on a platform with a sniper rifle in his hand. Safety lines connected him to two crossbeams, which meant Runeclaw didn't have to feel bad about attacking him.

The man looked up as the muffled sound of the drone reached him. Runeclaw blasted him before he could react, throwing electricity out of his tail to encompass the man and holding it there until his target slumped. Amber circled the drone around the unconscious figure once as if to confirm he was down, then headed for the roof.

Runeclaw reported, "I don't see any guards on the roof."

Scarlett replied, "They must've counted on that guy to handle overwatch. There might be cameras, I suppose. Anyway, we're pretty much committed at this point." The drone swooped down over the roof but didn't stop.

Runeclaw leapt off into the cover of a huge air conditioning unit. "Ready."

Scarlett opened a portal, stepped across, and knelt beside him. They waited for a reaction, but none came. Using magic above the building hadn't set anything off, as they'd hoped.

Amber reported, "I don't detect sensors on the roof, only cameras. They might have noticed the drone, or they might not have. Either way, you're good to go."

Scarlett cast a veil to obscure them, and the Witches crossed over to the roof. Amber directed them into position. Each team aligned with a window in the building's ground floor since the second story had none. They would have to deploy in waves since there weren't enough windows to accommodate them all at once. Runeclaw would be in the first wave, right behind Scarlett.

Scarlett carefully lowered herself down the side of the building, hidden by a veil, then froze while Amber used her sensor pack to scan.

The infomancer reported, "No alarm on the window."

Scarlett used a small tool to cut a hole in the glass, then unlocked it and lifted it. She swung inside and waited while other Witches breached other windows and for Runeclaw and Lin to join her.

All around were the trappings of money and executive power. They included a large wooden desk, glass cabinets that had doubtless once held awards and mementos, and an array of expensive furniture. She idly wondered why they didn't take the stuff when they moved out.

At Wren's command to proceed, she opened the door and looked outside. The pricey carpet and additional glass cases lining the corridor wall confirmed she was in the building's management section.

Amber loaded a floor plan onto her display glasses.

"This is from the original construction records. The interior has most likely been altered since then, so I don't know how accurate it is now. Better than nothing, probably."

Thermal images popped onto the display. One set was the Witches, and the other had to be their enemies. Many of them were gathered together in the largest room. Scarlett asked, "What's that big place?"

Amber replied, "The studio. They had live audience stuff back in the day, which I guess required a lot of space."

Wren advised, "Only two entrances to that room and only two ways to get there. Expect guards."

Beside Scarlett, Lin muttered, "Not a good sign."

Scarlett replied, "No. Especially since there might be innocents inside the studio with them, so we can't do anything useful like blasting in from the top."

Someone on another team whispered, "Enemy spotted."

Scarlett stuck her head around the corner and spotted a guard down a medium-length hallway at another corner. "Here too." The man's rifle in his hands pointed directly down the hallway toward her. "If they're smart, they'll have eyes on their forward guards from around the corner, so if they go down, they'll know they're under attack."

The building's layout made that an obvious tactical choice, and once they were out in the open, they'd still have a significant distance to travel to reach the studio. It was an ugly scenario.

Wren asked, "Anyone have a bright idea?" The comms remained silent. Then she added, "The Spell Riders are fifteen minutes out, but I don't think we can wait for them."

Lin replied, "I agree. These jerks might have roving patrols. It would be stupid for them not to. Better to take the fight to them when we choose rather than letting them force us into it."

A couple of the other Witches agreed. Wren ordered, "All right, then. We go in fifteen seconds from mark."

The countdown appeared in Scarlett's display. She asked, "Do you want to take the shot?"

Lin grinned, drew the crossbow from her right thigh, and pulled back the string. "Definitely."

Runeclaw interjected, "Try not to screw this up."

The drow snorted. "Thank you for your support, fur face."

"Always happy to help."

When the clock reached zero, Lin pulled both triggers. The bolts shot out and struck the guard in the chest, where he had body armor, and in the neck, where a small patch of skin was exposed. He reached up and grabbed for the dart. Then his eyes rolled back in his head as he crumpled.

Scarlett hissed, "One down. Go, go, go."

CHAPTER TWENTY-SEVEN

Scarlett rushed around the corner and found exactly what she expected and the thermal scan from her sensor belt had shown. Another guard was at the far end of the long hallway with his rifle raised. He pulled the trigger the moment she appeared, and Scarlett fell to the floor as bullets stitched the wall above her. She rolled and scrambled back around the corner and stood. "All-out run. Ready?"

Lin nodded, and Runeclaw replied, "Do it."

Scarlett stuck her wand around the corner and sent a blast of lightning blindly down the hallway, then raced after it. As she did so, she noticed something she hadn't seen before. Perhaps he had been hidden, but a man with a wand was visible beside the guard. He smiled smugly, then pointed the wand above her head and yanked it down.

Scarlett dove forward, almost crashing into Runeclaw as he accelerated past her. Lin yelped and landed on the floor beside Scarlett. The sound of the ceiling caving in behind them filled her ears.

Scarlett reached behind her back, drew her revolver, and did her best to aim through the dust. She fired two rounds as the material swirled out of the way enough for her to see what she was aiming at. The wizard went down with a yelp, and Lin blasted the other with a burst from her rifle. Runeclaw sent a long-distance lightning bolt at both of them to ensure they'd stay down.

Over the comm, Lin snapped, "Defense in depth. Be careful. They pulled the ceiling down." She looked at Scarlett. "Fast?"

Scarlett nodded. "As fast as we can. Hoof it before they can escape."

Ellis put a hand to his ear. "Repeat that?" A moment later, he walked to Camus and reported through the shield that protected the robes as they did their work collaring the new captives, "We are under attack."

The wizard's face twisted in the deepest rage Ellis had ever seen from him. "Can you and your people handle it?"

He responded with a sharp nod. "We are prepared."

The other man's expression lightened, but only a touch. "Good. If it becomes dire, interrupt us. Better to lose all of our remaining uncollared subjects than for any of us to be captured or killed."

"Understood." Ellis also understood that Camus was referring to the robes, not to the rest of them, although he hoped the man might feel bad if Ellis was among the lost. He stared around the room to ensure things were as they should be, then headed out the door closer to where the nearest invaders were.

A trio of guards stood in a rectangular room with their rifles pointed at the only possible entrance. Ellis had chosen each potential collaring location with a focus on defense, and his people had added more barriers to create long lines of sight and kill zones. It had been a ton of work to do it with multiple places, but he'd wanted to be prepared in case their best efforts at secrecy failed them, which they had. He snapped, "Status."

The team's leader replied, "We have attackers in both lanes. Ceilings are dropped. Some got through, but we blocked most of them. Cameras are down in that part of the building, probably because they're shooting them out as they reach them. Sounds indicate those behind are working on clearing the rubble while the others advance."

Ellis nodded. "Portal in reinforcements. I want all of these scumbags dead before they can reach the studio and interrupt the procedure."

Scarlett stuck her head around the corner, then leaned back to avoid the bullets that slammed into the wall. She snarled, "We've got another long hallway to deal with."

Lin replied, "Allow me." She reached for her belt, pulled the pins on a pair of grenades, and hurled them one after the other down the hallway. A moment later, a loud crash came, followed by screams of pain. "Flash-bang and frag. Great combination."

Scarlett shouted, "Run!" as she took off down the hallway. Her revolver was still in her hand, and she fired as soon as she saw movement in the next room. Her bullets struck two guards marching through a portal and dropped them both to the floor.

She took in the new arrivals as she shoved the pistol into its holster. They wore heavy body armor, which meant her center mass shots probably had done little more than knock down her foes. Heavy protection that looked like big motorcycle helmets covered their heads.

She snapped, "They're fully armored." She reached for a throwing knife and hurled it, then grabbed the other and threw it, too. The first took out an enemy, but the other clattered away ineffectually.

More opponents continued to enter the room through the portal, which seemed to have an endless supply. Lin fired her rifle in short bursts and sent the enemies into cover as soon as they arrived, but it wouldn't be long until they realized they had the better position and turned the tables on that plan.

Scarlett looked for the magical maintaining the portal but saw no one. She cast a slick of ice on the floor under the new arrivals' feet and cursed as they moved more slowly but held their balance. Then the bullets came, and she dove for cover behind an equipment console filled with old machines. Sparks flew as metal met metal. She snarled, "That armor is going to be a problem."

Runeclaw countered, "Armor won't help them against lightning." He snuck into the tiny area between the end of the equipment rack and the far wall, aimed, and fired a wide blast of lightning from his tail. It spread as it went, quickly growing wide enough to encompass all the attackers. Then it hit an invisible shield and fizzled out before it could reach them.

Runeclaw growled, "Shielded," and dashed forward. He wanted to run through the portal, find the magical holding it open, and take him out of the fight. That approach could strand him on the other side and take him out of the battle, which was unacceptable.

As he advanced, one of the guards noticed him and fired at him. Runeclaw's mind automatically calculated the angle and noted that recoil would push the incoming bullets along a certain path.

He angled in the opposite direction and took stock of his opponent as he reoriented and charged. The helmet wasn't joined to the armor, but most of the time it created a more or less seamless barrier with it to protect the neck, one of his favorite targets. Runeclaw would have to knock his target's head around to expose it, which was possible but potentially challenging.

Armor plates covered his foe's forearms, upper arms, thighs, and shins, but only in the front. He smiled inwardly at that discovery and changed his angle yet again. One of his best skills was attacking from an unexpected direction. They had anticipated and protected against a frontal assault.

He hurtled between the legs of the man who was shooting at him, spun, and slashed his claws across the back of the man's calves. Muscles tore just above where his boots ended, and the man let out a high-pitched scream that was muffled by his helmet as he went down.

Runeclaw sprinted toward the next closest enemy but had to dodge to the side to avoid getting kicked as another moved into his path. He snarled, leapt to the interloper's shoulder, and slammed his body into the side of the man's head. It moved enough to expose his neck, and Runeclaw slashed his claw across the pale flesh. Blood spurted as he jumped away.

He ran back toward the protection of the equipment racks as bullets chased him. "Okay. That armor sucks. They suck. This whole place sucks."

Scarlett laughed despite the danger. "That, my friend, is an understatement. Lin, how about another flash-bang?"

The drow replied, "Grenade out." A moment later, a sound like thunder filled the room.

Runeclaw blasted electricity at the nearest enemy, and he went down.

Scarlett snapped, "Their shield's down." She grabbed a flash-bang from her belt and tossed it through the portal. Lin's grenade followed a moment later. Scarlett's went off, and as the portal started to close, Lin's detonated and sent fragments in all directions. One of the soldiers yelled under his helmet and fell forward with blood welling from the back of his unarmored legs.

Scarlett took advantage of the momentary disorientation to blast them all with lightning. Lin joined in, and so did Runeclaw, raking them to ensure everyone got a dose.

After several seconds, they were confident the enemies wouldn't get up. She snapped, "Push forward before they run."

Ellis watched the brief battle through the doorway, then retreated into the large studio. He pointed at a pair of nearby guards. "You and you. Aim at the door. If it opens even an inch, hose it down."

The men moved into position without delay. He stomped back toward the ritual circle in the center of the room. A voice spoke in his earpiece. "The second group is through the barrier."

He snapped, "Do what you have to do, but do not let them get here. We've got the witch coming from the other side, and I'm gonna make sure she doesn't escape this time." He lifted his rifle, pointed it at the door, and waited for his opportunity to end the threat once and for all.

CHAPTER TWENTY-EIGHT

Scarlett pointed at the far door. They had to go through that bottleneck, and the enemy knew it. She whispered, "You blast it off its hinges. I'll send lightning through, then we run."

Lin nodded. "Ready when you are."

Wren spoke over the comm. "We are bogged down. Slight delay."

Scarlett replied, "How long?"

"Too long for you to wait."

Scarlett grimaced. "Okay, Lin. Do it." A wave of focused force magic blasted out from the drow's clenched fist and the door shattered into pieces that flew into the room beyond. Scarlett raced into the room behind a continuous blast of lightning, then skidded to the floor as bullets stitched the air over her head.

She took in the scene in flashes as she rolled and searched for cover. Her lightning had accomplished nothing since several men with rifles stood in its path.

Bullets struck the floor behind her as she moved and looked for options.

The studio room was huge, with equipment and prop pieces pushed back along each wall. A grid of pipes hung overhead, with a couple of large lights attached. Cables that had been attached to equipment but no longer were snaked out from the wall. Guards were clustered in each corner, all reacting to their intrusion. She waved her wand and pulled objects from around the room to create a barrier to the bullets coming her way.

Her gaze found the focal point of the room, dead center. Inside a three-layered ritual circle stood four captives. One was in the center of five bald men. Each of the latter had their hands on the collar around the captive's neck. Their magic caused the metal to glow and reflect off the layers of shields that protected them.

Scarlett reached for her revolver, then remembered it was empty. She snapped, "Center."

Lin had followed her into the room and was on the floor a dozen feet away behind a tall, rolling metal ladder. She replied, "On it." She rose to her knees and pointed her rifle at the bald men, but it was immediately ripped from her hands. An instant later, Lin's pistols flew out of their holsters.

The drow grabbed her reloaded crossbow and fired a bolt into the center area, but the magical field stopped it after a moment. The darts were able to penetrate skintight shields, but nothing bigger.

Scarlett drew Fang with her main hand and one of her knives with her off hand. She cast through the enchanted knife, continuing to summon objects around the room to provide protection as she charged at the guards. They had stepped forward to interpose themselves between her and the center circle. Bullets slammed into her improvised shields, and as they failed, she hurled the objects into the defenders ahead of her.

The barrage stopped as the men backpedaled, more from shock than any damage, she was sure. Scarlett used the distraction to wade in among them. She stabbed the first one she reached through the elbow, eliciting a sickening squeal as the man grabbed his wounded arm and went down to the floor.

Her follow-up slash struck a helmet and failed to penetrate, but it moved the man's head aside enough that she saw a flash of skin. Scarlett whipped Fang across the pale patch to deliver a shallow cut and a dose of the tranquilizer drug.

The next one depressed the trigger on his rifle, but Scarlett was already inside his guard, having used the man she'd just dropped as a shield. She whipped her left hand around to knock the barrel out of line and toward another group of guards, then stabbed him in the leg above his armor plate with Fang. The blade sank deep, and he collapsed a moment later as the drug did its work.

Scarlett waded through a couple more with similar results, then Fang spoke in her mind and warned her only one dose of the tranquilizer remained.

She shoved the sentient dagger into its sheath and drew her other knife.

A grenade clattered on the floor as Lin yelled, "Grenade out." When it went off, the smoke was confined to a force bubble around it.

Motion from the center caught Scarlett's eye as a portal opened and a collared captive was thrown through. Other robed men pulled the next captive into place. She snarled, "We have to get through that shield."

Lin replied, "Use the backpack."

"We'll lose our protection against the bullets."

"Do it."

Scarlett grabbed the lanyard and yanked it.

Runeclaw had taken down two guards with stealth attacks, ones far enough from other enemies that his efforts wouldn't be noticed. Now, he charged into the ring as its protective shield came down. He leapt onto the back of the nearest man in robes, reached up, and clawed his scalp from eyebrows to the back of his neck. The man screamed and batted at him, but Runeclaw was already in the air toward the next.

This one had turned at the other's scream, so Runeclaw landed on his chest instead of his shoulder. He dug in his claws, pulled himself up, and raked at the man's throat with his claws. His foe lowered his chin, so Runeclaw opened skin and flesh, but nothing vital. A hand swatted him away, and when he landed on the floor, he immediately surged into motion again.

A flash of crimson robe caught his attention, and he vectored toward it and leapt into an attack, only to be met by the swinging end of the man's staff.

Runeclaw flew out of the circle, landed on the floor, and slid out of control across its smooth, painted surface.

He fetched up against a guard's foot, momentarily stunned. Fortunately, it took the man longer to raise his foot and stomp than for Runeclaw to return to himself and dart out of the way. He jumped and slashed his claws across the back of the man's thighs above his knees and hit the floor around the time the man did.

He ripped his claws across the man's forehead to make blood flow down his face, then charged toward the center ring again, intent on paying the man in the crimson robes back for having the audacity to strike him.

Scarlett finished off her current opponent and turned toward the circle in the center. She only managed a couple of steps in that direction before a fusillade of bullets slammed into her. She felt them like punches raining down on her chest and back, then striking her arms she lifted them to protect her head. Her knives fell from her hands in mirror images of one another as she fell.

The backpack's anti-magic emitters had taken several hits and protected her from damage but at the cost of its existence. Magic snapped back into being like a rush of adrenaline to the brain.

Scarlett drew her wand, slammed magic into her muscles to keep herself upright, and wrapped tight force shields around the wounds on her arms. She reached down to her boot to draw her second wand and threw magic around with both hands. Her first efforts were all about protection, tearing objects from the walls and pipes from the grid above to put in the path of the bullets seeking her, Lin, and Runeclaw. She snapped, "Lin."

"Go."

"Put a force shield over the ring. Be ready for some weight."

"Got it."

Since the other team hadn't arrived yet, everyone except the three of them and the innocents in the center were combatants. Inspired by the defenses they'd used, Scarlett pointed her wand at the roof above a corner filled with guards, focused her will, and ripped the ceiling down on top of them. The destruction cascaded along that side of the building and dropped metal, wood, and stone on the men gathered there.

Wren shouted, "Nice work, we're in."

As the chaos in the studio ratcheted up, Scarlett saw the protective force shields around the ring fall. "Into the center, now." She used her wands to grab the two remaining uncollared captives and pulled them away from the rest.

Runeclaw dashed in and slashed one of the bald baddies across the back of his ankle. He cried out and fell, then flopped on the floor as a bullet fired from elsewhere in the room struck him in the head.

Scarlett grabbed a dart and hurled it at the retreating robed men but missed as their enemies fled through a portal. Lin fired her other crossbow dart, and Scarlett thought she saw it hit one of them. Then the portal collapsed, and they were gone. Scarlett slumped to the floor as the adrenaline rush left her and put her head down. "Little help here. My arms aren't working too well."

Lin knelt beside her and trickled a healing potion into her mouth. A couple moments later Scarlett was back up. Half of the studio's ceiling had collapsed, and some bad guys escaped, but the Witches freed two captives. She asked, "Do we know the robe who died?"

Lin shook her head. "I checked. We don't."

Runeclaw ambled over. "No casualties, only some injuries. No one important got hurt."

Scarlett rolled her eyes. "It's good that we can always count on you to add insult to injury."

Runeclaw grinned. "I'm always here for you, Scarlett."

"Gee. I'm so lucky."

Wren's voice sounded loud in her ear. "Everybody out. I don't trust the structure of this place. Get." A moment later, they had all portaled back to their motorcycles, and shortly after that, they were all safely back at the warehouse.

CHAPTER TWENTY-NINE

Camus paced the length of his basement, treading the same path repeatedly. His mind teetered on the infinitesimal line that separated control and a complete lack of it. The bottom of his battle staff slammed into the floor with each second step as he used it to display his frustration.

He could imagine no way anyone could have discovered the collaring ritual given the preparations in place. None at all—unless someone had spilled the secret. But Ellis' plans had been designed to prevent that, and Camus agreed they were adequate.

He remembered the sight of the witch as she arrived in the television studio and the rage that had filled him in that instant. He'd stayed focused on his task and trusted the guards Ellis had deployed to deal with the witch and her allies.

They had done well until the roof came down. That unexpected move had unsteadied the other robes enough to lose control of the protective shield around the ritual circle. This left only one practical option—to flee the battlefield.

Camus snarled inwardly at the thought. Fleeing was not something a leader did. Fleeing was not something *he* did.

A scuff of a shoe on the stone floor caused him to spin and march toward the men who had arrived. He'd sensed them coming down the stairs. Ellis was in the lead, with two others behind, all in dusty battle gear. One of the men had a bandage wrapped around his neck. Camus snarled, "How." It was a demand, not a question.

Ellis stood straight as he shook his head. "Unknown. Our security was tight, and the location wasn't revealed to the others until the last minute. This should have been impossible."

Inwardly, Camus raged at the choice of words. Obviously, it had been possible since it had happened. Outwardly, his tone took on an icy edge. "A leak among your people?"

Ellis' head shake was emphatic this time. "No. It can't be. But we are the three who knew where it was before that final hour."

Camus shifted his gaze to the others for the first time. Both men, both terrified. Ellis looked stressed as well but didn't display the same fear. His expression had an edge of acceptance as if he knew he deserved whatever he received.

The Luminous Veil's leader stomped up to one of the two guards. He looked him in the eyes from a few inches away for several seconds, then demanded, "Did you reveal the location to anyone?"

The man shook his head and opened his mouth, but no

words came out. Camus responded with a thin smile. "Let's be sure." He put his hand on the man's head and summoned his magic.

A moment later, a spell washed over the man. Camus was dimly aware of the guard screaming as his mind crashed into the other man's consciousness. That was an outward concern, and his focus was inward.

He sifted through the man's thoughts and recent memories in search of anything that tasted like guilt. His examination was thorough and complete, but he had found nothing by the end. Convinced of his innocence, Camus released the man, who instantly collapsed to the floor, unconscious. "He knew nothing."

The other guard's eyes widened as Camus stepped toward him. Ellis moved out of the way but stayed close enough to protect Camus from a physical attack. Camus repeated the process he'd used a moment before, touching the man's forehead and sifting through his thoughts one by one. He was distantly aware of more screaming, but it still held no relevance to him. The man collapsed when he released him. "He knows nothing either."

His eyes locked with Ellis'. The other man nodded as if giving him permission to test him. Camus shook his head. He knew Ellis was loyal. The spells he'd already woven around the man without his knowledge would have warned him of any potential betrayal. "Very well. I believe you. It wasn't you or your people. Damn that witch and her friends."

Camus resumed his pacing, shoving his stick into the floor loud enough to echo in the space after every second step. Ellis waited for him to turn and come near before asking, "What now, sir?" His expression suggested that Camus' behavior had alarmed him and might still concern him.

"I need you to get the other robes and their assistants to the plateau four hours from now."

Ellis' head bobbed. He was relieved to have a task. "What should I answer when they ask why?"

Camus growled, "Tell them their leader commands it." He cast the spells to open the entrance to his secret chamber, stepped through, and collapsed the opening before Ellis thought of following.

The atmosphere in Wheels was cautiously relaxed. No locals were present, but the place almost overflowed with Witches and Spell Riders, all of whom seemed to be having a good time. If someone had looked closer, they would have noted that everyone was armed, additional armaments of a heavier variety were cached around the room, and no one overindulged in anything that might dull their senses. Wren had ensured they were ready for a reprisal from the Veil before she allowed everyone to relax.

Scarlett thought the Witches' leader might hope they tried it. She felt the need for some payback, too. Other matters required her attention before she could consider how to accomplish that.

She was seated at a round table with pizza boxes in the center that she shared with Lin, Runeclaw, and the two people they'd rescued. The tall, thin man was named Pete, and the blonde with the sculpted cheekbones and startling green eyes was Clara. Each had a hand on Runeclaw, who lay between them on the table.

Scarlett took a sip of her root beer and looked at Lin. When the other woman nodded, Scarlett asked, "So, you two, what can you tell us?"

Pete spoke first, his voice halting as he told his tale. "I was snatched off the street. Three men. They threw me into a van. I managed to punch one of them." He seemed proud of the accomplishment.

"Then someone stabbed me with something when the van started to move, and I was out. I woke up in a holding place, but we weren't there long. We moved a couple of times through portals."

Lin replied, "One right after the other?"

"Sometimes we'd stay in a place for a while. I kind of lost track of time."

Clara interjected, "I think they kept us drugged. Something in the food or the water. It's all really hazy."

Pete added, "Then we got to where we were going and stayed there for a while."

Scarlett asked, "Do you know where that was?"

Clara answered, "It was in the woods. Small cabins."

Lin asked, "Fancy?"

Pete snorted. "No. Not at all. Old. Musty. Gross."

Scarlett drummed her fingers on the table and worked to control her frustration. "Who was there with you?"

He replied, "Men with guns, always. Sometimes all dressed up for a fight, other times just in black clothes. Different men in robes, sometimes, too."

Lin asked, "What did they do to you?"

Clara replied, "Made us sleep."

"Really?"

Pete nodded. "Yep. Made us sleep."

Scarlett and Lin had agreed not to share their thoughts while the kids were still there, so she noted that response for later. "What happened before we arrived?"

Pete answered, "The wizards applied the collars to some of the others."

"How?" She hadn't had the opportunity to notice what was going on during the fight.

Clara replied, "They stand all around with their hands touching the collar. Then it moves through the person."

Surprised, Scarlett asked, "What?"

Pete explained, "It goes all fuzzy and moves right through their neck. When it's normal again, it's on."

Lin remarked, "That's why we didn't see a seam. Jerks. What happened then?"

Clara shrugged. "They opened the gate and pushed them through."

Scarlett asked, "Is there anything else you can tell us that might help?"

Pete shook his head, but Clara looked thoughtful. After a moment of quiet, she replied, "There was one thing someone mentioned that I didn't understand."

Pete laughed darkly. "Only one thing?"

Clara amended, "Okay, a lot of things. But one stood out. They're going to be gathering something."

Scarlett asked, "Gathering?"

Pete's expression turned thoughtful. "Right. I remember hearing that word. Gathering."

Scarlett looked at Lin again, and the other woman shrugged. She didn't have any more useful questions, either. "Good work. Have another slice of pizza and finish your soda, then we'll get you to the hospital so you can be checked out for safety's sake."

Once that was accomplished, she and Lin discussed it at the bar. The drow commented, "I'm sure there are tons of small camps in woods all over the place. Amber can try searching for it, but that's unlikely to pay off. Just not enough information."

Scarlett replied, "Maybe they own it through shell companies or whatever. That could be a lead."

Lin countered, "Or maybe it's deserted and they're squatting."

Runeclaw was lying on his stomach on the bar in front of them. "I'm sure they wouldn't have been stupid enough to leave a trail to that place."

Lin observed, "The sleeping had to be so the captives could have other magic applied to them, don't you think?"

Scarlett nodded. "I'm sure that's it. To ready them for their collars."

"It would make sense to knock down their resistance some beforehand."

Runeclaw asked, "Do you know how to do that?"

The other woman shook her head. "No. But clearly it's possible."

Scarlett ran her fingers through her hair in frustration. "What could they still have to gather? It doesn't make sense. They're done with the collaring. They got all the captives they needed unless our taking those two hampered them. What else could it be?"

Lin shook her head. "I can't even begin to guess."

Wren stepped up between them and put a hand on each of their shoulders. "Where is it?"

Scarlett turned her head to look at her. "Where's what?"

The other woman tapped her ear. "I was listening in. Magic, you know. Where's the gathering?"

Scarlett stared at Lin as facts lined up differently in her head, then shook her head. *Not gathering, but a gathering.* "I don't know, but I think we'd better find out, and fast."

CHAPTER THIRTY

After several hours of meditation, Camus' internal clock alerted him that the meeting with the other members of the Veil on the plateau was imminent. He banished the protection of his ritual circle, rose from his cross-legged position, and moved to his wardrobe.

He removed his robe, then checked to be sure his wizard grenades and healing and energy potions were in place. He reached into the wardrobe, retrieved his serpentine poison blade, and slid it into the sheath at his belt.

Before donning the crimson robes again, he inspected the armor to ensure it wasn't damaged. It was pristine, as usual. He checked the mirror to ensure the robes covered every hint of the armor's presence, then took a deep breath, turned, and left his secret chamber.

Ellis was waiting outside, standing in a relaxed position opposite the door in newly cleaned body armor. Pistols rode both of his hips. Camus nodded his approval of his subordinate's attentiveness. "Everything is ready?"

"Everything is ready." Ellis' tone was grim.

In contrast, Camus was beginning to feel buoyant about taking another step in the right direction. "Good. Let's go." He used his battle staff to draw a circle in the air, and a portal appeared with the plateau on the opposite side.

The moment his feet touched the earth on the other side of the portal, he felt the power underneath reach out to him, recognize his magic, and entwine with it. He stopped, breathed in, held the breath, and exhaled. He repeated the cycle, feeling more powerful with each passing moment.

Ten minutes later, the other attendees arrived as three portals opened simultaneously. Emerald Robe stepped through the first, with two assistants trailing him. Turquoise Robe came through the second, also with two at his side. Gold Robe emerged from the last one with only one helper.

The new arrivals moved until the four groups were in a rough diamond shape. Each watched the other groups with veiled or not-so-veiled aggression.

Camus looked at Gold Robe with satisfaction. He looked strong, which meant the healing potion he'd received after the battle had counteracted whatever poison the witch and her friends might've hit him with inside their last-minute dart. It would have been a shame for him to miss this.

Emerald Robe demanded, "What is this?"

Turquoise added, "Who compromised the collaring ritual? Was it your minions, Crimson?"

Without answering, Camus extended his senses, which

were already tied to the essence of the place. He detected heavy shields on Emerald and Turquoise but only token defense on their assistants. Gold Robe had protected himself and his assistant with strong force shields, and Camus had done the same for himself and Ellis before the others arrived.

He smiled, slipped a hand into his robe, and came out with one of his wizard grenades. Camus lifted the glass tube. "I wanted to show you this." He tossed the vial into the center of the space.

It broke open when it hit the ground, and shimmering sand spiraled into the air, glittering as it twisted and twined. It seemed like a narrow whirlwind was drawing it up toward the sky.

Camus twitched his staff when it had stretched to a continuous line about twelve feet tall. The sand whipped instantly into frenzied motion, becoming a tornado that ripped across the plateau. It encompassed the spot where Turquoise and his people stood, then Emerald, then Gold.

When it was over, his and Gold Robe's were the only assistants left standing. The other four had been torn to shreds, their bleeding bodies contributing to the plateau's power reserve.

Emerald Robe and Turquoise Robe reacted by stumbling backward and producing wands they pointed at him. Camus calmly asked, "Will you let me into your minds to ensure you have not betrayed the Veil?"

No answer came. Camus looked first at Gold Robe, who hesitated but managed a firm nod. He then looked at Emerald and discovered the other man was staring at Turquoise.

Turquoise growled, "This is a violation."

Emerald added, "You have no reason to doubt us."

Camus shook his head. "I have every reason to doubt you. You have just provided it. Ellis." In his peripheral vision, he saw his subordinate pull his right-hand pistol and shoot four times. The anti-magic rounds drilled into the arms and hands that held the wands, both of which dropped to the ground.

Camus used his magic to float the wands to himself and spun them in the air as he examined them. "Inferior work." A gesture shattered the magic items, and the pieces fell. Another gunshot sounded suddenly, and Turquoise's head snapped back before he fell. Camus looked at Ellis.

The other man shrugged. "Backup wand."

Camus nodded, then turned a smile on Emerald Robe. "I guess you'll have to enjoy all the pain I had planned for both of you. Don't worry. I'll keep you alive long enough to fully appreciate it."

Some time later, only Camus, Ellis, Gold Robe, and the latter's assistant remained on the plateau. The bodies of Turquoise Robe, Emerald Robe, and their assistants had all been absorbed into the earth.

Camus walked to Gold Robe, who had watched everything in silence, and put a hand on the man's shoulder. "You would've let me look because you had nothing to hide, as I expected. One or both of them had been attempting to modify the collars in a way that would have undermined the Veil's goals. And not well enough to remain undetected."

The other man nodded. "I am as I have always been. Loyal to the Veil. And to you."

"It's good to know I have one person I can truly trust." He smiled and used the man's name to emphasize how important that connection was to him. "Kingston."

THE STORY CONTINUES

The story continues with book eight, *Witch's Wrath*, coming soon to Amazon and Kindle Unlimited.

Claim Your Copy Today!

AUTHOR NOTES: TR CAMERON

JULY 22, 2024

Thank you for continuing on to the author notes! I hope you enjoyed this one. I liked writing it, although it was a challenge for some reason to keep it flowing. I think the strongest thing about this one was the dialogue. Maximum snark.

Every now and again I read books with a first person perspective, particularly the Dresden Files since it's Urban Fantasy. I think the Anita Blake books might be first person too, though I haven't read them in a while. In any case, I'm of a mind to try it someday, though probably not with Oriceran books. My major hurdle though is that I really like writing villains.

Like, a lot. I'm sure there are ways to bring out in dialogue and the MC's internal monologue all the things that I would have brought out in a scene from the villain's POV, but I'm not quite sure how.

I'd love to write from a Villain's perspective. Scalzi's *Starter Villain* does that really well, though I'd want to be…

nastier. Comedy, plus torture and stuff. On second thought... maybe I should stay in my lane!

I attended the Midwest Writing Workshop in Muncie, IN. It was a nice getaway from my normal life and a chance to be in the author headspace exclusively for a few days. I enjoyed the experience. The panels weren't right for me, though, which happens. I don't think I'll be back, but I would encourage anyone interested in authorness who's nearby to check it out. Really looking forward to Killer Nashville next month.

The kid and I are headed to Erie, PA for a little unstructured away time this week. The beach on Presque Isle, some miniature golfing, maybe some escape rooms, and a really cool spot where someone has converted cars into sculptures in their (very large) front yard.

Niall Horan's show was phenomenal. We had such a good time, and really liked the opener, Del Water Gap, too. The Justin Timberlake concert, though was unlike any I've ever been to. The technical elements and choreography were so impressive. I've got a background in live television, so I have a particular affinity for visual tech. And this was just... awesome. The live DJ set beforehand was also really cool. We're considering going again when he's in Pittsburgh, more for the experience than the music.

August we've got Hozier and maybe Ice Nine Kills. September is a lot for us. We've got concerts galore. I've loved Green Day forever, and the bill includes the Smashing Pumpkins, Rancid, and the Linda Lindas, all of whom I like. Avril Lavigne should be so fun. Weezer is a longtime favorite. Sisters of Mercy is more for me and my wife, but we're bringing an adult friend, and the kid is coming too. Toronto again for Conan Gray. Barenaked Ladies, unless the kid opts for Sleeping With Sirens (I'm hoping not), and then finish it up with Twenty-One Pilots, who I've become a little obsessed with. I could see us following them to Detroit the next night, even though we're seeing them again in October.

Yeah. September is busy. LOL

TV has fallen off a little of late. We're continuing with *Doctor Who*, now in the first Jodie Whittaker season. There are a couple Sarah Jane Adventures with Doctors 10 and 11, so I think we'll grab those eventually, and will start *Torchwood*, a Dr. Who spinoff, when we're all caught up. I'm interested in *The Acolyte*, and catching up with *The Boys*.

Not much theatre action lately, either, other than *Despicable Me 4*, which we enjoyed more than expected. Looking forward to *Twisters* and *Deadpool & Wolverine*.

I'm re-listening to the *Black Jewels* series in audio. It's one of my favorites of all time, and always a pleasure to revisit. Anne Bishop. Highly recommend. Her newer series is also wonderful. Like I do with Jacqueline Carey, I read whatever Anne Bishop releases. I'm also listening to *American Gods*, which I both read and watched, and it's not getting me. I don't love the narration. I'm sure it will, eventually. And still working my way ever so slowly though *Dune*. Epic Sci-Fi is very wordy. On the page, I'm re-reading the Sword of Truth novels. I have a real love-hate relationship with them. Some of the ideological elements are just so unsubtle. But it's a strong, well-written story.

I'm going to make an effort to be more active on social media in September. I do fun stuff. I should share it. Plus, I have cats, so pet pictures are abundant.

Time for me to sign off and get moving on book 8.

Until next month, joys upon joys to you.

Standard monthly reminders - If you're not part of the Oriceran Fans Facebook group, **join**! There's a pizza giveaway every month, and Martha and (usually) I and all sort of fun author folks show up via Zoom to chat with our readers. It's a great time, and the community feel to it is truly fantastic. The group is very welcoming and enthusiastic. Oriceran Fans. Facebook. Your phone is probably within reach. Do it!

Before I go, if this series is your first taste of my Urban Fantasy, look for "Magic Ops." I promise you'll enjoy it, and you'll like Diana, Rath, and company. You might also enjoy my science fiction work. All my writing is filled with action, snark, and villains who think they're heroes. Drop by www.trcameron.com and take a look!

Your monthly reminder that you can find the free prequel short story for The Nomad Witch series, "Vacation Day," here: https://dl.bookfunnel.com/rxccsvm5jn

PS: If you'd like to chat with me, here's the place. I check in daily or more: https://www.facebook.com/AuthorTRCameron. Often, I put up interesting and/or silly content there, as well. For more info on my books, and to join my reader's group, please visit www.trcameron.com.

AUTHOR NOTES: MARTHA CARR

AUGUST 13, 2024

I've started a project answering questions for my son about my life. I realized after the most recent fifth round of cancer, and then chemo this time, that he was expecting me to die sooner rather than later. It's been a lot for him to deal with and there isn't much I can do to make it better, except tell him stories that I can leave behind – eventually. Hopefully, a long time from now. I'm going to let you guys listen in as well.

My author notes right now are going to be answers to questions and all of you can get to know me better, too. Maybe inspire, maybe give you a laugh along the way.

Today's question is: What are some of your favorite sayings?

I have a few sayings that I remind myself of all the time. 'What is mind cannot be taken from me.' 'This or something better.' Those are two of my favorite go-to's. There's one though that I trot out when I'm tired, worried, overwhelmed and stuck. That one is, 'God bless [fill in name of someone here] right where they are, change me.' The shorthand is 'God bless [name], change me.'

I've used that one on constant repeat at times to remind myself what is mine to change and what is none of my business. Almost everything is none of my business. Sometimes, things that directly concern me are none of my business. If it's about someone else there had better be a specific question someone asked me, and then I'm hopefully only answering that question and not adding in pearls of wisdom on the sly.

For me, when I'm grinding on something that's probably not actually happening, it just could happen, and therefore has no solution because I can't change the future till it gets here, I look around for distractions, like minding your business. Sometimes, I'm not even aware I'm doing it till I'm knee deep. Sometimes, I'm aware of it but think I'll get special compensation this time because clearly you would benefit from my unsolicited advice. I mean, who wouldn't? None of those situations are going to go well in the long run.

The goal here is to learn to sit with what's actually bothering me and make friends with the feelings. Too woo-woo for you? Well, as a veteran practitioner of avoidance for some decades, I can tell you that denial or avoidance or repression works really well, till it doesn't at all. Then, even when it's working it takes a toll on the body and erodes friendships but at such a slow pace you won't see it for a long time when there's real repair work on both that needs doing. Scars will be left behind on both.

The alternative is to do nothing. To feel whatever is coming up. That's it. Just let the feelings sit there and teach me something. Instead of pushing them away because it felt like they must be a bellwether of something going wrong (rarely), or were too much of a reminder of what I'd done wrong in the past (not exactly), I let them be and wondered what they might be here to teach me.

This is harder than I'm making it sound even when it looks obvious and simple to everyone around you. It's painful and the brain will think up a hundred excuses why it would be better to look away but instead, I just sit with it. I even like a good visual, that's the writer in me, and I picture this amorphous creature sitting next to me on a bench, sharing some tea. In other words, this feeling isn't the enemy, it's a necessary teacher.

It usually takes me a few days to a couple of weeks but eventually I spot the message and I'm always amazed. Some detail in the pattern of behavior or memories that changes everything. Like noticing how I put up with a lot of bad behavior and never got angry. It wasn't safe when I was a kid and by the time I was an adult, it was second nature to act like everything was fine. The consequences for me was a lot of constant stress, and continued bouts of cancer. Last round my oncologist said offhandedly, "The recurrence was probably brought on by stress." Time to change.

Back to that saying. The first part of it is to make sure I don't cause harm when I'm in that place, finally willing to sit still and be somewhat patient. It's also so I don't distract away from whatever revelation is on its way to me. The second part is to open myself up to the idea that this process is all about change, and for the better.

The first few times I did this, or maybe the first fifty, it was white knuckling all the way even with a tribe of people around me to encourage and cheer me on and share their stories, which was super helpful. However, here I am about twenty years into this process and my entire life has changed for the better and it's possible for me to get to some of the darker layers and just be. Not easy, but doable and eventually I get to the other side. The payoff comes when I notice myself speaking up when someone crosses my boundary, or I say no to something because of the way I'm being treated instead of just putting up with it, or when I take that big swing even if I'm afraid and start a new project full of promise and I'm not stopped by the possibility of failure. Airing out a lot of that anger has left me with a sense of calm that I'll figure it out and if I can't I'll find someone to help me. Subtle change, maybe, but also life changing. Bonus payoff, it's given me space to let others off the hook too. I no longer need people to be a certain way so I'm comfortable or feel safe or at least less anxious. I can regulate myself because there aren't emotions pinging around inside here that I'm desperately trying to corral and repress. I let them out, let them be wild for as long as they needed to, looked at all of it - with some help, and found out I'm okay. That's gold to me. Love you. Love, Mom. More adventures to follow.

OTHER SERIES FROM T.R. CAMERON

Urban Fantasy
(with Martha Carr and Michael Anderle)

Federal Agents of Magic (8 book series)
Scions of Magic (8 book series)
Magic City Chronicles (8 book series)
Rogue Agents of Magic (8 book series)
Witch Warrior (12 book series)
Secret Agent Witch (8 book series)
Secret Agent Witch (8 book series)

Science Fiction
(with Martha Carr and Michael Anderle)

Azophi Academy (4 book series)

OTHER SERIES IN THE ORICERAN UNIVERSE:

THE LEIRA CHRONICLES
CASE FILES OF AN URBAN WITCH
THE EVERMORES CHRONICLES
SOUL STONE MAGE
THE KACY CHRONICLES
MIDWEST MAGIC CHRONICLES
THE FAIRHAVEN CHRONICLES
I FEAR NO EVIL
THE DANIEL CODEX SERIES
SCHOOL OF NECESSARY MAGIC
SCHOOL OF NECESSARY MAGIC: RAINE CAMPBELL
ALISON BROWNSTONE
FEDERAL AGENTS OF MAGIC
SCIONS OF MAGIC
THE UNBELIEVABLE MR. BROWNSTONE
DWARF BOUNTY HUNTER
ACADEMY OF NECESSARY MAGIC
MAGIC CITY CHRONICLES
ROGUE AGENTS OF MAGIC

OTHER SERIES IN THE ORICERAN UNIVERSE:

OTHER BOOKS BY JUDITH BERENS

OTHER BOOKS BY MARTHA CARR

JOIN THE ORICERAN UNIVERSE FAN GROUP ON FACEBOOK!

CONNECT WITH THE AUTHORS

TR Cameron Social

Website: www.trcameron.com

Facebook: https://www.facebook.com/AuthorTRCameron

Martha Carr Social

Website: http://www.marthacarr.com

Facebook: https://www.facebook.com/groups/MarthaCarrFans/

Michael Anderle Social

Website: http://lmbpn.com

Email List: https://michael.beehiiv.com/

https://www.facebook.com/LMBPNPublishing

https://twitter.com/MichaelAnderle

https://www.instagram.com/lmbpn_publishing/

https://www.bookbub.com/authors/michael-anderle

BOOKS BY MICHAEL ANDERLE

Sign up for the LMBPN email list to be notified of new releases and special deals!

https://lmbpn.com/email/

For a complete list of books by Michael Anderle, please visit:

www.lmbpn.com/ma-books/

www.ingramcontent.com/pod-product-compliance
Lightning Source LLC
LaVergne TN
LVHW041923070526
838199LV00051BA/2706

9798888784907